CROSSDRESSING:
SENT TO GIRLS BOARDING SCHOOL

© 2010 Jo Santana

The right of Jo Santana to be identified as the Author of the Work has been asserted by him in accordance with the Copyright, Designs and Patents Act 1988.

First published in the United Kingdom in 2010
by Miro Books

All rights reserved. No part of this publication may be produced, stored in a retrieval system, or transmitted in any form or by any means, without the prior permission in writing of the publisher, nor be otherwise circulated in any form of binding or cover other than in which it is published and without a similar condition including this condition being imposed on the subsequent purchaser.

All characters in this publication are fictitious and any resemblance to real persons, living or dead, is purely coincidental.

ISBN 978-1-906320-26-3

Typeset by Miro Books
Printed and bound in the UK & US
A catalogue record of this book is available
from the British Library

Cover design by Miro Books

CROSSDRESSING:
SENT TO GIRLS BOARDING SCHOOL

JO SANTANA

CHAPTER ONE

I was moving my stuff into my sister's old room while Mom and Dad were away for the weekend and Sarah was visiting her friend Ellen. My parents had said we could do the swap, Sarah was going away to boarding school at the end of the summer break and her room had an ensuite bathroom. Our parents would be away travelling on business and said she preferred to stay at school during the weekends and breaks, whereas I planned to get home as much as possible, so she wouldn't have much use for her bedroom and we decided to swap. I dumped my computer on her desk, my desk now and looked for somewhere to start hanging my clothes. I opened the door to one of the closets and it was still full of her clothes, dresses, skirts, tops and coats. Damn, she still hadn't cleared everything away, I guess I'd have to do it for her. I went and looked in the chest of drawers, sure enough, panties, bras, pantyhose and a pile of other filmy feminine garments. Ok, I'd have to move it all to her new bedroom. On an impulse I went back to her closet and looked at her clothes hanging there. I picked up a frock and took it off the hanger, it was a shirt style dress in heavy black silk, with embroidered three quarter sleeves and buttons up the front. I remembered her wearing it at a party, she'd looked so pretty, how could she not want to take the dress with her?

The impulse hit me and I tried hard to resist, I knew I shouldn't, but I had to see the dress on me. Sarah was a year younger than me but by some quirk of genetics was half an inch taller, people often mistook her for my elder sister. Fortunately we were both quite skinny, no matter how much either of as ate we didn't put on any weight, which may have been good for a girl but it sure wasn't for a guy making his way in the world of Brad Pitt and Dwayne Johnson. But it did mean that I'd fit into the dress without any problems, except that of course I didn't have anything up front. I went back to the drawer and found a bra, stuffed it with pantyhose to give it shape and fastened it on my chest. I felt like a little kid playing with his mom's clothes, but maybe it was more than that, already I felt something quite new, a warm, comfortable feeling, almost as if this was right. My new shape stuck out in front of me, it sure looked good enough in the mirror. I started to close the drawer and saw a matching pair of panties. Why not? I pulled them out and stepped into them. I checked myself again in the mirror, yeah, not bad, time to try the dress.

I put the cool black silk over my head and pushed my arms through the sleeves, when it was on me I buttoned up the front and went to look in the mirror. Christ, I did look good, a bit of makeup and long hair and I'd be a good looking girl. I laughed, this dressing up could be fun. I decided to leave Sarah's stuff in the closet after all and manage with just the other closet for my own clothes. Then I had another thought, if anyone saw me like this they'd think I was some kind of weirdo, a transvestite or maybe a homo. That wouldn't be good, I'd need to leave town if that happened. Maybe I'd better get out of this stuff quickly, but even as I thought it, I felt so good dressed as a girl that I decided to keep it on for a bit longer while I moved my stuff. After all, with no-one in the house there was nothing to lose. I went back to my old room and packed some stuff in a box and carried it through to my new room and started putting it all away. I went to switch on my computer and found that I'd left the cables in the old room so I went back again and unplugged them from the wall. I took a look around, it seemed that I'd moved everything to my new room so I was virtually done. I plugged my PC in, booted up and got online.

"Who are you?" a voice asked from the doorway, shit, it was Sarah's voice. I spun around and she was standing staring at me with her friend Ellen.

"Good Lord, it's Andrew. Why on earth are you wearing my clothes?"

They were both smiling broadly, probably more at my beetroot red face than the dress I was wearing with my artificial tits thrusting out the bustline.

"Er, well, I just wanted to see what it looked like on me. There's nothing wrong with that, is there? Besides, you were going to abandon this stuff so you didn't want it any more. You've borrowed my clothes in the past, what's the difference?"

"You're right, Andrew, there's no difference," she said soothingly. "It doesn't bother us, it's just that your face is as red as the paint on the front door."

"Look, I didn't expect you back yet, could you go out and I'll get changed."

"No, please," she said. "Don't change, you look sweet in my dress, there's no-one else here and we've already seen you so keep it on. What do you think, Ellen?"

Her friend, Ellen Campbell, nodded. "I agree, he does look good in that dress, in fact I think it looks better on Andrew than it ever did on you."

"See? Don't change, Andrew, stay as you are, we won't tell anyone."

Eventually I agreed and carried on sorting through my new room. I even forgot I was wearing girl's clothes, when Sarah and Ellen went down to get some lunch they fixed some for me and called me down. Still wearing the dress I went downstairs into the dining room. To my utter horror, Ellen's boyfriend Adam Murdoch was sitting at the table. I went to rush back upstairs but Sarah was ready for me.

"No, Andrew, don't worry about it, Adam is in on the secret, he won't tell either."

I wondered bitterly if half of Portland, Oregon was in on the secret.

"Hi, Andrew," he said with a small smile. "I like your dress."

"Shut up, Adam. I was only trying it on out of curiosity, the girls persuaded me to keep wearing it."

"It's ok, it looks good, chill out man. It makes no odds to me, but don't expect me to ask you out," he grinned.

I ignored the barb and started on the plate of food that Sarah had put in front of me.

"Hey, Andrew," Ellen said to me. "Sarah and I had an idea, make the weekend more interesting. You spend the weekend as Sarah and she'll spend the weekend dressed as you."

I shook my head. "No way, Ellen. After lunch, I'm changing into my own clothes, I'm not looking for any more surprises."

Sarah was quick to protest. "Please don't do that, I was looking forward to being you for the weekend."

"You can do that anyway, I'll lend you some of my stuff."

She shook her head. "That won't cut it, Andrew, I won't feel like you if you're still in your normal clothes. Please, do it for me."

The others joined in and pressed me hard to agree.

"Well, I suppose I might. I think I could regret it, though."

"No, you won't," Sarah said emphatically. "You'll love it, we'll both love it, isn't that right, guys?"

Ellen and Adam both nodded.

"Ellen, would you give me a hand to sort out Andrews's clothes and I'll get dressed?"

"Of course," she said.

"Andrew, while I'm doing that, would you tidy away the dishes? You'll find my apron behind the kitchen door."

Before I could make a bitter reply, they were gone.

"I'll check the TV schedules," Adam said. "While you're clearing the dishes I'll see if there's a film for us to watch this afternoon."

He left the dining room and I went out to the kitchen and found Sarah's pretty floral PVC apron. I cleared the dining table and loaded the dishwasher, then wiped over the kitchen and tidied away the food they'd left strewn everywhere. I looked around, it seemed pretty clean to me, I was about to join Adam when Sarah called down from upstairs.

"Andrew, would you come on up and help us."

I realized I still had Sarah's apron on so I untied it and

hung it up. When I got upstairs Sarah was wearing a pair of my denim jeans, black Converse sneakers and one of my Ralph Lauren button-collar shirts. She'd put on my black leather Minority Report jacket with the mandarin collar, her hair had been gelled and tied at the back in a ponytail and she'd removed all of her makeup. I was quite startled, she did look very much like a guy.

"Yeah, that's excellent, Sarah, you look real good. Why did you want me?"

"We need to finish off your outfit, Andrew, do your hair and makeup. Come into my bedroom, well, your bedroom now, and we'll do the rest for you."

"Makeup? No, that's not part of the deal. I'd look stupid."

Ellen took my arm and led me into the bedroom. "You won't look at all stupid, Andrew. In fact you've got a lovely face that will look much better with a little makeup. Think about it, suppose someone did see you by accident as you are now, they'd know you were a guy n a dress. We need to do the makeup to complete your disguise."

I didn't like it, I grumbled and moaned but they pushed me to sit down on the bed and while Ellen plastered my face with pungent smelling cream, eye makeup, lipstick and heaven only knew what else, Sarah took care of my hair. It must have taken them half an hour before they were satisfied.

"Put these pantyhose on your legs, Andrew, you can't

be me without them."

I pulled them up and she helped me get them over my waist.

"Just these shoes, they'll look nice with the dress."

I had to stop it there and then. "Christ, you can't be serious, they're high heeled shoes, I can't walk in those."

They both laughed. "Of course you can, we girls do it all the time. Come on, put your feet into them and you can take a look in the mirror."

I got the shoes on and stood up, then nearly toppled over. They caught me just in time.

"Don't worry, you'll get used to them. Come and see how it looks."

I wobbled over to the mirror and looked at the reflection of a pretty young girl, no, a very pretty young girl. Sarah stood to one side of me, she looked convincing too, a nice looking guy, if a little on the feminine side.

"You've done a good job on me, you're right, at least I don't look like a guy in a dress. Thanks both of you."

They smiled. "Andrew, why don't you go downstairs and join Adam," Sarah said. "He's all on his own, Ellen's going to help me sort my new room out, we'll be down in half an hour or so. Watch your heels on the stairs, you need to hold the rail."

"Yeah, I'll be careful, I'll see you both in a bit."

I wobbled carefully down the stairs and into the lounge. With each step I got more confident at walking in heels, it wasn't so hard after all. Adam was mesmerized by the pretty young girl that sat opposite him.

"Andrew, that is truly amazing. If I didn't know it was you, I might even make a pass at you, I'm glad I was in on the secret."

"All credit to the girls, they did it for me. What's showing on the TV?"

There was a re-run of an English movie, Love Actually. Total and utter nonsense, some sort of Christmas tale about, well, love. We sat and watched it, later Sarah and Ellen came down and joined us.

"Are you looking forward to going to New York, Adam?" Sarah asked him.

"Yeah, I am. I've only been for a couple of short visits, it's so far away. The idea of spending three or more years there is great, Portland is so quiet most of the time."

"What about you, Ellen?"

"Me too, yeah, I agree with Adam, I can't wait to get out of Portland and see some life for a change."

"You're really lucky, what about you, Andrew, are you looking forward to it too?"

I had to think about that for a moment. The truth was I that I regretted I'd ever applied to go to New York. I loved my home, the state of Oregon, the city of Portland. I'd applied for Columbia in a fit of misplaced enthusiasm when I thought that exploring the bright lights and big city would be a life changing experience. Now I wasn't so sure.

I tried to explain it to them, Adam could hardly believe it.

"I thought you were dead keen on going, Andrew. Is it too late to change your choice of college?"

"Yeah, much too late, I'll just have to be miserable and put up with it."

We watched the movie but we'd all seen it before and it got boring. Adam wanted to take Ellen out for the evening.

"Look, we can grab some pizza or something, maybe take in a decent movie, a couple of beers afterwards. What do you say, Ellen? I'd ask Sarah and Andrew to come with us, but obviously they're not exactly dressed for it."

"Oh, but they are," she replied. "Sarah looks just like a boy and Andrew like a girl. Who the hell would know?"

"Hey, come on, guys, you know I couldn't do that," I shouted.

"And why not?" my sister asked me. "As a matter of fact you make a very pretty girl, if anyone needs to worry it's me, I'm not half as convincing as you are. Look, Andrew, dressed and made up like that, you really are a girl, there's nothing to suggest otherwise."

I looked down at my crotch.

"Well, almost nothing," she laughed. "You're not going to be displaying that around the town, are you?"

"That's it, then," Ellen said. "Let's grab our coats and go. I'll help Adam clear away while Sarah sorts Andrew out with a coat and purse."

I'd been outvoted, I went with Sarah to the hall closet and she found me a lightweight cotton raincoat to go over my dress.

"Before you put it on, Andrew, I'll do your nails, it won't take long. Come back upstairs with me."

I followed her up the stairs, still wobbling precariously in my heels. I sat down on the bed again and she made me hold out my hands.

"Hmm, there's a tiny bit of hair on your hands, I'll get rid of it for you."

To my horror, she got a pink Ladyshave razor and shaved all of the fine hairs from my hands.

"Yep, that's better, hold your fingers out straight and I'll varnish the nails."

Ten minutes later I was staring at my newly pink nails, waiting for them to dry. Sarah found a black evening purse and filled it with the things I would need, money, tissues, my house keys and cellphone.

We went back down the stairs, me clutching my purse in one hand and the rail in the other. She helped me into the black raincoat and buttoned it for me and fastened the belt, the buttons were the wrong side and totally unfamiliar to me. She stood looking at me critically.

"I reckon a pretty scarf would brighten up your outfit, hang in there."

She came back with a silk scarf that was a riot of colors and fastened it around my neck.

"Wait there one second, we're nearly done."

She reached up and clipped silver dangly earrings to my ears and then a tiny matching necklace around my neck.

"You need a couple of bracelets really, I've got these for you."

When was this ever going to end? She fastened two bracelets to my right wrist and strapped a silver cocktail watch to my left wrist.

"Hmm, something's still missing, I know what it is, wait there."

She ran up the stairs and came back with a perfume bottle. She applied it to my wrists and neck, so much that I thought I'd faint with the odor, I was standing in a cloud of pungent smelling perfume.

"That's it, Andrew, you're ready to go."

Thank God for that. Adam and Ellen came out to join us with their jackets on.

"There's one more problem," Ellen said.

"Yeah, what's that?" I asked her. I could think of at least ten, maybe more.

"We can't call you Andrew, neither can Sarah use her name if she's a boy. You'll have to swap names."

"That's ok with me," Sarah said. "What do you think, Sarah?"

Who? Of course, I was now Sarah.

"It's ok, I can do that, Andrew."

The girls both smiled and we went out to Adam's car.

"Girls in the back," my sister said.

I waited for her to get in, but she just looked at me.

"Oh, ok, I forgot, sorry." I got in the back with Ellen and the 'boys' climbed into the front. We drove into town and walked along to find a diner. My sister said that she would act as my 'boyfriend' and persuaded me to take her by the arm as we went along the sidewalk.

"You ok, Sarah?" she said to me.

"I'll tell you when we get home," I replied quietly. In truth, I was very embarrassed and totally terrified. Yet I felt something else too. Was it possible to actually enjoy cross dressing this much without being a weirdo? To feel so good about being a girl, outwardly, at least?

CHAPTER TWO

I'd known beforehand that my trip into town would literally be a night of terror, but my sister and Ellen did work hard to make me feel comfortable as a girl. We ate pizza, went to a movie where I sat and trembled with fright as my sister put her arm around me as if I was her girlfriend, I guess I was her girlfriend for that evening. They insisted that we went to a bar where there was some music and a small dance floor, my 'boyfriend' showed me how to dance properly as a girl and I had to smile when I caught sight of guys looking me over. I knew what that look was, I'd worn it on my own face when I'd been out on the town, appraising the local females, except that now I was on the receiving end. When we got home it wasn't over, the girls helped me remove my makeup, clipped up my hair and I was given a nightdress to wear to bed, a short white cotton shift imprinted with teddy bears, of all things. I even had to wear matching teddy bear patterned panties. I got into bed and my sister came and sat on the bed to talk to me.

"Thanks for helping this weekend, Sarah. I'm having a great time as a boy, are you enjoying it as much?"

I thought for a moment. "Yeah, I think I am, you know. It's a lot of fun."

When I awoke I remembered who I was supposed to be. I put on 'my' pink dressing gown and went downstairs for breakfast. My sister was already up, wearing jeans and a T-shirt as Andrew. She smiled a good morning to me.

"I enjoyed our date last night, Sarah," she said to me. "I hope you did too."

"Yeah, as I said to you last night, it was a lot of fun."

"Could you get us some breakfast, juice and cereals would be nice?"

I looked at her sharply. But she was waiting for me, she stared back. The meaning was clear. 'Get me my breakfast, girly'. I sighed and went into the kitchen, got everything out and laid the dining table for four. By the time everything was ready, Ellen had come downstairs and Adam joined us shortly afterwards.

"I really envy you guys," my sister said.

"Why's that?" Ellen replied.

"You're all going off to New York for a fantastic experience at Columbia and I've got to spend a year stuck in a girl's boarding school in Oregon. You'll be having a great time while I'm on my own back here. It's just not fair."

"Don't be so sure," I said to her. "I'm not really looking forward to going to New York at all, I think you're lucky staying in Oregon."

"If you think that, why don't you stay and let your sister go with us instead?" Ellen said.

I stared at her. "Believe me, I'd be more than happy to, Ellen. If it wasn't for the problem that she's seventeen with a year of senior high school to finish and I'm eighteen and need to start working for my degree. If I stayed here, it would be too late for me to change universities and anyway, my sister is too young and unqualified to get into Columbia."

"So why not swap places, Sarah? That would be simple."

I realized that I was still Sarah for the rest of the weekend and she was talking to me. I laughed at her.

"I've just explained, she's too young and unqualified. Besides, I haven't got anything else fixed up."

"No, I meant literally swap places. You become Sarah at Karen Hall Academy for Girls in Spokane and she can become Andrew at Columbia in New York. Sarah hasn't been to Karen Hall before, she's been attending school in Portland, so they don't know what she looks like."

What couldn't Ellen see?

"Look at me, Ellen, look at my sister. I'm a guy and she's a girl, even if we wanted to, we're different."

"But other than that, you would, then?"

It was irritating me now, going on and on about the same thing. I wanted to move on and talk about something interesting.

"Yeah, I guess so, why not?"

Ellen and I, the 'girls' cleared the dishes. After I'd showered, they helped me with my female clothes, hair and makeup. When I was finally dressed and made up, we went downstairs, I was wearing two inch heels this time and a pretty floral print dress so that I felt much more comfortable, less wobbly than on the high heels the night before. When I glanced in the mirror I was horrified, my hair was shoulder length and they'd tied it in bunches with slides and ribbons.

"Jesus Christ, I look like a girl," I snarled at them.

They grinned back.

"Isn't that the point?" Ellen asked.

"Oh, yeah, I guess it is, sorry."

Adam took us out for a drive in his car and we stopped at a diner for lunch. I was getting more confident now although the stares from other guys at this pretty girl walking past them both unsettled and amused me. Afterwards we went to an amusement park and my 'boyfriend' took me on several rides. I did my best to play the part and it seemed that I was doing ok, Ellen and my 'boyfriend' told me I looked totally normal, just like any other girl. Prettier than a many of them, too.

We collected a takeaway for dinner on the way home

and they got me to serve it up in my floral apron. I was quite used to it by now, had it only been yesterday that all of this had started? As I was taking off my apron, Ellen and my sister came out to the kitchen.

"Sarah, would you and your brother come into the hallway for a moment?"

"Yeah, sure, what's up?"

"Nothing, just come and look. Stand side by side in front of the mirror."

We did as she asked, then I asked her what for.

"What do you see in front of you, Sarah?"

"Me and my, er brother, I guess, a guy and a girl."

"Ok, and who's the girl?"

"Well, me. At least, on the surface, obviously, but…"

"That's the point, Sarah, you're just a girl on the surface, like any other girl, so why can't you do it for your sister, swap places? You said you'd like to stay in Oregon, she wants to go to New York, it would be the perfect solution."

We argued for some time but the thought of being dressed like this and staying in a girl's boarding school with a lot of other girls was terrifying. My sister pointed out that I was already thinking like a girl, talking about 'other girls' and that the transition would be almost effortless, but I couldn't face it. The whole idea was monstrous, totally bizarre, how on earth they thought it could ever work was beyond me. Our parents were due back the next day and I was at last allowed to remove my makeup and get out of my feminine clothes. I knew that I'd be pleased to get back to normal, at least I thought I knew, but when I removed my bra and panties and pulled on my pajamas, I missed the feeling of the filmy, feminine garments and considered for a moment wearing my nightdress and matching panties to sleep in, but the thought of the teddy bear pattern clinched it and I stayed in my pajamas.

Mom and Dad came home the following day and life got pretty much back to normal. I didn't forget my cross dressing experience and often looked in the closet at the dresses and skirts to be reminded that I'd really done it, and enjoyed it. Our parents went away on Friday again, this time for a week and they agreed that Sarah's friends could come round and stay, Ellen and another girl, Hannah, with whom she was going to Karen Hall Academy for Girls with, in Spokane. Adam couldn't come, he was away staying with relatives so I was in the house with three girls. Late Friday evening after we'd had a few drinks, Sarah and Ellen told Hannah about my cross dressing experience last weekend.

"I'd love to have seen that," she grinned. "Andrew, how did you look?"

"He was really pretty," Ellen said, jumping to my defense.

"I don't believe it, there's no way a guy could look good in a dress and makeup, they always look gruesome."

Maybe it was the drink, but I jumped into the discussion.

"Not always, Hannah, Ellen is right, I did look pretty good, prettier than any of you girls look."

There was a stunned silence.

"Prove it, then," she said.

My sister and Ellen glanced at each other, then at me. I'd unwittingly thrown down the gauntlet and there was no taking it back. They literally dragged me up the stairs and made me strip off and put on panties and padded bra in the bathroom. I came back into my bedroom and they'd prepared my clothes for me, it had all happened so quickly. How much had I had to drink?

"Hey, I'm not sure this is a good idea."

"Be quiet, Sarah, you can't let Hannah get away with calling you a liar, can you?"

"Well, I guess not," I said doubtfully.

They pulled a floral dress over my head and I pushed my hands through the long sleeves. It came down to just above my knees, Ellen handed me pale, flesh colored pantyhose and I rolled them up my legs and over my waist, she handed me white strappy shoes with a three inch heel and a t-bar strap on the front. They pushed me to sit down on the bed and they started on my hair and makeup, my sister finished my hair first and started on my nails, then clipped on my earrings and necklace, bracelets and watch. They finished and I stood and looked in the mirror, they'd done another fantastic job. The girl that stared back at me was, well, very pretty. The amazing thing was, I loved it, loved being her, although it would be very dangerous to admit it.

"Would you spend the weekend as Sarah again, it'll be good because I'll be able to be Andrew? Please say you will."

I gave it long enough to maintain my dignity and then, pretending protest, nodded my head. They smiled broadly.

"You'd better go down and see what Hannah thinks now, Sarah, we'll follow you down in a moment," Ellen said.

I went down the stairs and into the lounge, Hannah was watching the TV while we'd been upstairs. She noticed me out of the corner of her eye.

"Yeah, hi Sarah, you ought to watch this, it's pretty good. How's Andrew doing, not so good I imagine?"

"Hannah, look at me."

She looked across. "Yeah, ok, why? What's…holy shit, is that you, Andrew?"

I nodded. She came and sat next to me and looked at me closely. "It's amazing, you really are gorgeous, you know. I'd never have believed it."

She shook her head. She looked me over, asked about my clothes and makeup as if it was the most normal thing in the world. I realized that she was just treating me like another girl, nothing to get excited about once the initial surprise had melted away. We sat next to each other, she held my hand and looked directly into my eyes.

"So will you be coming with me to Karen Hall Academy for Girls, Sarah? I wouldn't mind if you did?"

"That's a silly idea, no way would I ever get away with it."

"You would if I helped you, Sarah. Why don't you give it some thought?"

My sister and Ellen walked into the room at that moment. Although she looked once more like my brother.

"Yes, why not, Sarah? Hannah would help you, you could stay in Oregon like you want to and I'd get to Columbia with my friends.

I felt at that moment that the world was spinning the wrong way on its axis.

"Look, all of you. Boys do not go to girl's schools, period."

"But you're not a boy, Sarah, you're a girl, look at you. What else could you be?"

I argued and protested, eventually they wore me down to the extent that I said I'd think about it. There was no way, no way on earth I'd do it but I just wanted to get them off my back and stop the argument that was getting too heated. I did agree to stay as Sarah for the whole weekend and found by Sunday night that being a girl became second nature. The following morning I woke up to a shock, during the night they'd moved all of Andrew's clothing out of my bedroom.

CHAPTER THREE

I banged on my sister's bedroom door. Ellen answered it, which surprised me.

"Ellen, where's my sister? I need to talk to her."

A head appeared around the door. "Sarah, what's up?"

"You know what's up, where are my clothes?"

"They're in your bedroom, of course," she smiled.

"Damnit, this is going too far. I mean Andrew's clothes."

"Ah, you can't have those, I'm Andrew, for the whole week, don't you remember?"

"No I don't, this was just for the weekend. Ellen, tell her what was agreed."

"You mean tell him," she said. I nodded wearily. "Ok, whatever."

"Andrew," she said, turning to my sister. "Sarah agreed to do this for the whole week until next weekend."

Andrew looked at me triumphantly. "There you are, it's the truth. Look, Sarah, you just had too much to drink, that's why you can't remember."

I thought back to that evening, I was sure it was the weekend, but I could be mistaken.

"Sarah, get yourself showered and your bra and panties on and Ellen and I will come and help you get dressed and made up. Don't worry, sweetie, you'll be fine."

Sweetie! I felt my anger rise as she said that, but I decided to let it go. As I turned to go back to my bedroom, Ellen handed me a small tub of cream.

"Before you shower, rub this all over the hairy parts of your body, it'll make them smooth. You need to let it soak in for twenty minutes, so sit on the toilet and read a magazine or something, it's what I do."

I mumbled an acknowledgement and went to my bedroom. I rubbed the cream on and looked for a magazine, the only thing I could find was Cosmopolitan so I took it into the bathroom and sat down to wait. Twenty minutes later, bored with reading professional tips on fashion, slimming and how to make love to a man, I got in the shower and washed the cream away. Incredibly, my body was smooth and hairless, like a close shave. I hoped to Christ it would grow back quickly after this week was over. I dried and dressed in my padded bra and panties and went into the bedroom, where Ellen and Hannah were preparing my clothes.

"Where's, er, Andrew?" I asked them.

"He's downstairs," Ellen replied. "We couldn't have him in the bedroom while you were dressing, could we, he's a boy?"

"Oh, I guess not, no."

They'd got out a pretty pink dress with large blue flowers printed on it.

"Sarah, we need to pinch your waist in a little, we'll put this basque on you," Ellen said.

As she was saying it, Hannah was pulling a satin, lightly boned basque around my body, she told me to breathe in while she fastened the hooks and eyes but when she was done I found I couldn't breathe out. Ellen looked at me carefully.

"That's definitely better, Sarah, although we may need a little more control, let's see how it goes."

It wasn't too bad in the basque, once I'd got used to my diaphragm being compressed. Ellen helped me to put my pink dress on and tightened the black patent belt around my newly narrowed waist. I glanced in the mirror, sure enough it did make my body look that slimmer and prettier. Both girls laughed.

"Come on, princess, let's get you finished," Ellen said.

They helped me pull on pantyhose and the white strappy shoes, this time while they did my hair and makeup I was told to paint my own nails.

"You'll need to get to know how to do it yourself,

Sarah," Ellen said. "Every girl knows how to make her fingernails look pretty, isn't that right, Hannah?"

She nodded. "Yep, quite right. You know, you were right, you're much prettier than any of us, I wonder what the secret is."

They finished my hair and makeup and let me look in the mirror. The narrowed waist and belt buckled tightly around it was so effective, it made my whole body look, well, girly. Very girly.

"Nice, eh?" Ellen smiled. "We'll get your jewelry on and we can go downstairs."

They gave me a chunky ethnic necklace to put on.

"You'll need to fasten it yourself, Sarah, you have to get used to it."

I managed to close the tiny clip, and then they gave me my earrings to clip on. Hannah held a small mirror while I sat on the bed and fastened them, when they were done Ellen was waiting with two ethnic bracelets and a chunky watch in a pink to match my dress. I stood up to look at the final result and saw a very pretty teenage girl in a pink, patterned dress, slim, the wide black patent belt dragging my waist in even more, adorned with tasteful ethnic jewelry. They'd put a pink flower to one side of my hair and two pink hair slides the other side. I shook my head in disbelief.

"It's pretty amazing what you've done, you two."

"So you like it?" Ellen asked.

I smiled at her. "I love it, thanks."

"I thought you would," she said. She looked at Hannah with a strange expression, then turned back to me.

"You can't keep using that hair removal cream, Sarah, I'll give you some tablets to take each day to stop the hair growing for now."

She went out of the room and came back with two tablets and a glass of water.

"Take two of these each morning and two in the evening, that'll stop it growing," I'll ask Andrew to keep you supplied.

"Like instant tanning pills, are they?"

"Something like that," she said as I swallowed the pills.

The weather was warm and we went out that afternoon, the four of us. Me, Andrew, Ellen and Hannah. We got the Trimet bus into town and Ellen and Andrew split up from me and Hannah. We walked arm in arm, two pretty young girls enjoying a relaxing stroll in the city centre. Hannah was a great girl to be with, I felt so pleased to have made friends with her.

"Have you any idea where the other two were going?" I asked.

She grinned. "Yes, and no, it's a secret really so I can't say anything."

I hoped to Christ it wasn't something to get me into yet more embarrassing trouble. We met up with them later and went for coffee. I noticed that I was the only girl in a dress, the others, well, Hannah and Ellen, were wearing jeans. I felt so feminine compared to the way they looked, I couldn't fathom why. After all, I was just dressing up, they were the real thing. But it was nice to be the prettiest girl in our group.

In the bar there was a piano playing and we ordered coffee. A couple was dancing on the floor, I watched them for a few moments and then felt a tap on my shoulder. I looked around, startled.

"Excuse me, Miss, would you like to dance?"

It was a guy, a good looking one, true, but a guy nonetheless. I looked at the others, horrified. They just grinned at me.

"Er, no, no, thank you. I'm fine."

"Ok, if you change your mind, I'm sitting over there."

He pointed to a table at the end of the bar, another guy was sitting there looking at us.

"It's just that," he mumbled as he continued to speak, obviously embarrassed. "You're so pretty, I thought I'd give it a try. Think about it."

He walked away and I could see my companions barely containing their laughter. We finished our coffee and I picked up my purse to pay for them. Even the waiter gave me the eye, this was getting over the top, I wondered how the hell I'd ever allowed myself to get into this.

"Come on, gorgeous," Ellen said to me with a smile. "Let's get the bus home before you break any more hearts."

I was bright red with embarrassment as we walked out of the bar.

Back home, it was time to eat. "Sarah, would you make us a plate of sandwiches, and bring us some cokes," Andrew said to me.

I stared at him. "Why me, why should I do it?"

"You're wearing the dress, sweetie, it's your job. We'll find a film to watch on the TV."

I put on my apron and bustled around the kitchen and made a plate of sandwiches, put them on a tray with four glasses and four bottles of cokes and served them in the lounge.

"Gee, sweetie," Ellen said. "This is really nice, thanks a lot."

"That's ok," I smiled, glad they appreciated me. I still had my apron on but it would protect my pretty dress so I kept it on as we ate. Afterwards I cleared away. Ellen and my sister were next to each other on one couch, I sat next to Hannah on the other.

"Sarah, you're enjoying being a girl, aren't you?" Andrew said suddenly.

"What? Why do you say that?"

"Aw, come on, we've all seen you admiring yourself in store windows as you walked past."

I nodded with embarrassment. "Well, yeah, I guess it is a lot of fun."

"That's nice. Look, we got you something to help you

while we were shopping this afternoon."

"What's that, then?" So this was their secret, I had to know what it was.

"It's a bit personal, we girls can go to your bedroom and we'll show you what it is."

I looked at Andrew, puzzled, but she smiled and nodded it was ok for me to go. I followed them up the stairs into my bedroom.

"Look, sweetie, we want you to lay on the bed, with just your legs hanging over the edge."

I opened my mouth to ask what the hell it was all about but Ellen looked at me sternly. "Please, Sarah, help us out here, just do what we ask, you won't be sorry."

I shrugged and lay on the bed.

"Close your eyes tight and don't open them," she said. I kept them shut and felt them removing my shoes and pantyhose, followed by my panties. Then it hit me, they could see my penis and testicles, the bits of me that were unquestioningly male. I started to jerk up but Hannah was ready for me.

"It's ok Sarah, just relax."

Reluctantly I lay back and felt Ellen pulling panties up my legs.

"You'll feel this, Sarah, it'll be a bit of a shock but just relax, and it'll soon go away."

What would soon go away, I wondered? Then I felt her grab my testicles and a burning pain shot through my lower body.

"Christ, that hurts, what are you doing?" I shouted.

Hannah held me down. "It's ok, sweetie, nearly there."

Ellen was tucking my penis into the panties and then she pulled them up completely and I could feel my penis tucked away firmly under my legs.

"You can get up now, take a look in the mirror," she said.

I winced as I got to my feet and walked across to the mirror.

"Lift up your dress and see, sweetie."

I lifted up the skirt of my dress and gulped, my male genitalia had disappeared. Where before they stuck out as a grotesque male lump from the front of my delicate panties, there was now a smooth, feminine shape.

"Where the hell has it all gone?" I asked them.

"Your testicles are pushed back into your body, it's quite normal, there is a space there that accommodates them," Ellen said. "Your penis is tucked between your legs and that's all there is to it, you end up with a female bodyshape. It's a special type of panty, called a gaff, designed to give you that smooth, female shape."

"But, I didn't want a female bodyshape," I protested. "Besides, it's sore, it hurts."

"That'll go away as soon as you get used to it," she said. "And as for not wanting a female body, well, you could have fooled me, Sarah. What do you think, Hannah?"

"Yeah, me too. I've rarely seen any girl look so nice, you're a real babe, Sarah."

The pain was starting to die away and my temper improved. "Ok, if you think it's necessary," I continued.

"It is," they both said adamantly. I looked at them suspiciously, but they appeared to be innocent of any further scheme.

"I'll wear it then. How to I take a leak?"

"It's designed to allow that, Sarah, no problem. You just sit down in the normal way and go."

I looked at her. "Normal for you, maybe."

She sighed. "And normal for you, Sarah, for heaven's sake, think like a girl."

"For this week, remember, that's it."

"Whatever," she replied.

I spent that week completely immersed in the look and the sub-culture of teenage girls. We went out, looked at stores, Hannah even persuaded me to try on a new dress in a small boutique. It was a very pretty party type dress we'd noticed in the window in satin material, purple with a large black pink bow tied around the waist as a belt. I was totally fascinated by it and trying to picture myself in it when Hannah asked me why I didn't try it on.

"I can see you're really taken with it, Sarah, go in and take a look."

"Yeah, I'd like to, but what if…"

"Don't be silly, I'll be with you and remember, you're

totally girl underneath, nothing to worry about."

We went in the store and the assistant found my size. I went into the changing room and to my embarrassment it was communal. Two other girls were trying on dresses, they looked at me dispassionately and then ignored me. I realized then that I'd thought of them as two 'other' girls. Other? I wasn't too sure about that, I seemed to have slipped into a gray netherworld, I wasn't entirely certain how I should think of myself right now, but I guessed it would have to be as a girl for the next few days anyway.

I was daydreaming and Hannah came into the dressing room, unzipped me and helped me put on the purple dress. She tied the sash and I checked it out in the mirror, it looked amazing. She saw my eyes shining and said I should buy it.

"I don't know, Hannah, it's a lot of money."

"Andrew won't mind, he said that there was some spare cash you should spend on yourself if you found something nice to wear. Why don't you just have it?"

I went out of the changing room and walked around the store, looking at myself from different angles.

"Yeah, I do love it, I'll take it."

"Great, I'll help you change back into your other clothes and the clerk can pack it ready for you."

I paid for my new dress and we made our way back to the bus. A sudden thought struck me.

"Hannah, I'm only doing this until the weekend, on

Sunday I go back to what I was before."

"Like Cinderella," she grinned.

"Exactly, but I shouldn't have bought this dress."

"Of course you should, you never know what will happen in the future."

CHAPTER FOUR

Ellen and Andrew made me try my dress on when we got home, they were both thrilled that I'd bought it.

"It's lovely," Andrew said. "Look, have you thought any more about us changing places at school?"

I hadn't and the answer was no anyway. "It's not possible, Andrew, really."

"Why not, you've been Sarah for most of the week, you've even been out and bought yourself a new dress. What's the problem?"

I couldn't explain it and didn't want to argue, I just knew it was impossible.

"Will you just stay as Sarah until the end of the weekend, then?" she asked me.

I looked at her suspiciously, they always seemed to have an agenda that I wasn't aware of. "When are Mom and Dad coming home?"

"Not until late Monday evening."

"Yeah, ok, I'll do that, then that's it."

Andrew leaned forward and kissed me on the cheek. "That's wonderful, Sarah, thanks. Have you had your pills this afternoon?"

I shook my head. "Ok," she said. "I'll get them for you now. We're going to have some fun this evening."

When she came back I asked her what we'd be doing.

"Ellen bought some bottles of wine and I bought some vodka. We're going to play a game of forfeit," she said.

Big deal. I said that sounded nice, then I went into the kitchen to prepare food for our meal.

We opened the first bottle of wine over dinner and I drank more than I should have. By the time we settled down to play cards, I was feeling quite merry. I lost heavily, my first forfeit was to wear my school uniform.

"What for, I never liked that uniform?"

"You've never worn it, Sarah, how would you know?" Andrew asked.

Oh yeah, of course. The new uniform that Mom and Dad had bought for Sarah to attend Karen Hall. He went to find the uniform while we waited. Did I think of Andrew as he? Well, yeah, I guess that was right, but it wasn't right. He came back with my uniform, a tiny dark red tartan miniskirt, white blouse, black shoes and tartan pantyhose. They helped me out of my dress and I put it all on with a lot of help. We played on and I lost again, this time I had to have my hair in pigtails with school color ribbons. They spent a few minutes working on my hair and we played on. I lost and had to put on my school blazer.

"Go and look in the mirror in the hall, Sarah" Ellen said. They came with me as I went and looked and saw a pretty schoolgirl in a short skirt and girly pigtails, tied with dark red ribbons.

"Yeah, so what? I'm just a schoolgirl, why shouldn't I look like this?" I said to them. They stared back, I couldn't work out why they stared for a minute, and then it hit me. "Oh, yeah, right, of course. But it still won't work so don't even think about it."

I kept losing, maybe if I'd had less to drink I'd have realized that something wasn't right. The next time they had me dressing in my school netball kit, short dark red pleated skirt, dark red full panties, white knee length socks, white trainers with pink trim, dark red polo shirt and a spare tabard that had been inadvertently brought home after a game. I looked in the hall mirror, yeah, really sporty, I pictured myself running around a netball court. The next time I lost I had to change into a dark red gymslip.

"We wear these during the week," Hannah explained. The headmistress likes us being dressed ready for either study or sport, whichever comes along."

I wore it over my white school blouse and had a dark

red sash tied around my waist. I looked pretty good in it, too. When I lost again, I had to change back into my short tartan miniskirt with the dark red pantyhose and white blouse, school blazer over the top.

"Isn't it time to finish up," I said wearily. "I seem to have lost every game, I'm getting tired."

"Two more hands," Ellen said. She dealt the cards and I groaned as I lost again, wherever my luck was it sure wasn't in the cards.

"You're running out of school uniform," Andrew laughed. "There's nothing left for you to try on. Except your school raincoat, I guess that will have to do."

He went upstairs with Hannah and came back with a long, full, navy blue raincoat. They helped me into it, buttoned it to the neck, buckled the belt and pulled the hood over my head and fastened the tab that held it closed.

"Very nice," Hannah said. "You're the sweetest looking schoolgirl I've seen wearing the Karen Hall Academy for Girls uniform and I reckon I've seen most of them."

They insisted that the forfeit required me to keep it all on for the rest of the evening. We watched a game show, Hannah sat next to me with our arms linked. I was thrilled to have such a nice girl as a friend. When the show ended I went upstairs, all of my uniforms were strewn on my bed and I hung them in the closet with my dresses, removed my makeup, put on my teddy bear nightie and panties and went to bed.

In the morning I had a giant headache. I went down to the kitchen in my dressing gown to find the others already there. Andrew gave me a glass of water with my pills and I got some aspirin to swallow as well. I wasn't hungry so I just fixed a glass of juice and went to sit in the lounge. They were looking at a bundle of photos.

"What are you all looking at?" I asked them.

They grinned at me. "Ellen took photos last night on her digital camera, we printed them out first thing this morning, take a look."

"Thanks, that sounds interesting."

I picked up several photos from the table and looked at a pretty teenage schoolgirl standing in our lounge. Then it hit me.

"Christ, this is me!"

"Of course it is," Andrew said. "Who else wore their school uniform last night?"

In picture after picture I was shown wearing sports kit, netball uniform, gymslip, the raincoat with the hood pulled up. Oh my God.

"Look, we've got to get rid of these, especially before tomorrow," I said desperately.

"Don't worry, we will," Andrew said. "Do you want the girls to give you a hand this morning to dress and do your hair and makeup? I expect you'll want to look especially pretty on a Sunday."

Why was she being nice to me, I wondered? But yeah,

it would be nice to make an extra effort on a Sunday. "I'll call down when I'm out of the shower."

I cleaned myself thoroughly and admitted to myself that I was really excited about which dress the girls would choose for me today. I put on my gaff panties, I was quite used to the technique now of tucking my testicles away and slipping my penis into the pocket that tucked between my legs. Then I went out into the bedroom. I needn't have worried lying on the bed was Sarah's, my, best white silk dress patterned with pale blue flowers and tied with a pale blue sash. I pulled on my flesh colored pantyhose, and they pulled the dress over my head. I put my arms through the sleeves and felt its gorgeous, soft, sensuous silk flowing down to my knees. They left me to tie the sash as they tidied my hair and makeup. It seemed to take longer this morning, they were obviously determined to make me look as pretty as possible. I slipped into a pair of white high heeled shoes with a thin strap, I was used to wearing heels now and the only thought that crossed my mind was how good they'd look with the dress. Then I looked in the mirror and smiled. I grinned as I twitched the hem of my dress, turning each way and then all around.

"I don't know what to say."

"We're glad you like it," Ellen said. "Why don't we go downstairs and join Andrew."

I tripped carefully down the stairs and we sat in the lounge, once again I noticed that I was the only girl in a dress. I glanced at the coffee table and saw that the photos of me in school uniform were still there, and then I turned as the front door opened.

"Hey, everyone, how's it all been?" said Mom. Dad was right behind her. They saw Andrew and smiled uncertainly, was this their daughter? "How's it all been dear? Hi, Ellen, Hannah. Sarah, is that you?" they said, looking at Andrew. Then they looked at me. "Who is this?"

The three of them looked at me, I felt my mouth opening and closing like a fish, my face glowing behind my makeup.

"It's your son, Mom. Didn't you recognize her?" Andrew said.

They stood gaping at me for several minutes. Dad came up and inspected me minutely.

"Is it true? It is you?"

I nodded. "Yes, it's true, Dad."

Andrew came to my rescue, or was it Andrew now that they were back?

"Ellen, would you and Hannah take Sarah upstairs to her bedroom and let me talk to Mom and Dad, it'll be a lot easier if I have a quiet chat. Go on, you girls leave it to me to thrash it all out."

As we left the room I saw Dad looking at the photos on the coffee table of me in all the different poses of my school uniform. He glanced back at me and sighed, then closed the lounge door. We sat in my bedroom, Hannah and Ellen did their best to make it right.

"I think I should change out of these things," I said miserably.

"It's a bit late for that, Sarah. Stay as you are, your parents are pretty broad minded, they'll understand," Ellen said. "Just be cool. Let me touch your makeup in, have you been crying?"

I nodded. "Yeah, maybe a bit."

They got out my makeup and helped to repair my face. Hannah tidied my hair and retied my ribbons, I felt better afterwards. She gave me a big hug and I felt that at least someone liked me, for whatever reason. The door opened and Mom was there. She smiled at the three of us, when she looked at me she was especially friendly.

"Hey, Sarah, don't worry about a thing. Come on down and we'll talk it all over."

I got up. "Mom, I can explain everything."

"I know you can, honey, but let's go down and talk between us all." She gave me a warm hug. "Ellen, Hannah, you come too, I expect Sarah will need all the support she can get."

Did she mean my sister, or did she mean me? I started to get worried.

"Mom, I really not…"

"It's ok, Sarah, we understand who you are, come on, Dad and Andrew are waiting."

As we walked down the stairs it struck me that they were still referring to my sister as Andrew. How could that be, couldn't they see through the way we were dressed? Dad was sitting down, he looked quite relaxed, I was grateful for that at least. Andrew looked quite comfortable too, I wondered what could possibly have been said to pour oil on the troubled waters of their two children swapping places. Dad asked Mom to do the talking. She smiled and asked me to sit by her. "That's a beautiful dress, Sarah, it looks lovely on you. Your hair and makeup too, I could hardly believe it was you."

I shrugged. "Yeah, well, it was, I don't know, it all just kind of happened, one thing after another."

"We looked at the photos, Sarah," Dad said. "I have to say you look good in your new school uniform, you must be looking forward to going to Karen Hall Academy for Girls with Hannah. I gather you've enjoyed your time there, Hannah."

"I have, Mr. Hague, it's a wonderful school. The girls are all fine."

"Good, good."

I was reeling, I couldn't understand what had been said. "Dad, it's Sarah that's going to Karen Hall Academy for Girls."

"I know you are, honey, that's right."

"But…"

Mom interrupted me. "Honey, we understand it all,

gender confusion is a fact of life sometimes, you're lucky, both of you, that you were in a position to deal with it by doing aswap. We'll do everything to support you of course."

I sat stunned by what I was hearing. Hannah sat next to me and took my hand, giving it a reassuring squeeze. She leaned over and spoke quietly. "We'll have a great time, I'll take care of you, don't worry."

I was numbed by disbelief. Dad was talking to 'Andrew' as if he'd talked like that a thousand times before, discussing the high spots of New York City while Mom listened on, smiling and nodding.

"Mrs. Hague, would you like Sarah and me to get coffee and serve it with some biscuits?" she asked.

"That would be fine, dear. You two girls go and do that."

Mom patted me on the hand and I got up, still stunned. We went into the kitchen and Hannah gave me my floral apron to put on.

"You make the coffee, Sarah, you don't want to spill it on that lovely dress so you'll need to wear your apron, I'll get the snacks."

While I was bustling around the kitchen getting cups and saucers while the coffee was brewing, Mom came into the kitchen, smiled at me and gave me another hug. "Sarah, my darling, I really wouldn't have believed it, but seeing you making coffee in your pretty apron I do believe it now."

She turned to go back to the lounge. "Mom, you shouldn't believe it," I shouted desperately.

She gave another of those 'wise mom' smiles. "It's ok, you do look beautiful, my darling. It'll work out fine, you'll see."

I served coffee in the lounge and kept my apron on so that I didn't spill any on my dress. I realized once more that I was the only girl wearing a dress, even Mom was in jeans. I looked around the room as I sipped at my coffee, Dad was talking earnestly to Andrew. Mom was asking Ellen about her plans to stay in New York City. Hannah nudged me. "Sarah, I think we're being ignored. Can we go up to your bedroom and do some Internet surfing on your computer?"

"That's a good idea, honey," Mom said to me. "You two girls go now, I'll come and check on you later."

CHAPTER FIVE

Hannah went home in the afternoon and I spent some time in my bedroom trying to get my head around some kind plan to resolve this crazy situation. Mom called me down for dinner and we sat at the dining table as a family, the four of us. Just as it always was, except that it wasn't. Mom made me put my apron on and help her serve the food onto the table and then we sat down to eat. We were silent for a few minutes, no-one seemed to want to break the silence. Dad tried an opening conversational gambit. "Are you looking forward to going to your new school, honey?" I was asked again.

Sarah, before I became Sarah, had attended a local senior high school for the first year, but when Mom and Dad announced that they were going to be traveling abroad for the next year, the obvious choice was Karen Hall Academy for Girls which Hannah had already attended for a year as a boarder. But now, he was talking to me.

"Dad, Mom, I'm not sure I want this, I don't know how it all happened."

Dad smiled sympathetically. "That's only to be expected, honey. Your mom and I do try to be modern parents, you know. We looked all this gender stuff up on the internet this afternoon, do you know what the first thing they said about it was?"

I shook my head.

"They said that people that were going through it were always confused and unsure at the start. I'll bet you feel that way too, don't you, Andrew?"

The male looking face of my new brother adopted a serious expression. He was wearing another Ralph Lauren button collar shirt, this time with a narrow tie. "I sure do, Dad, it's not an easy one. But I can tell you that both of us will sort out the issues in no time and be happy in our new lives."

I was shaking my head, but Mom put her hand on my arm. "Honey, we're trying to be twenty first century parents, and this has opened our eyes. To be honest, we're both thrilled that we've got the chance to help you both deal with a modern problem, we feel like we've got a new lease of life. Imagine, I'll be able to take my daughter out and show her all the things I showed her before, but this time it will all be new. As will Dad, with Andrew."

As they talked on, they grew more and more enthusiastic.

With a growing sense of disbelief I realized that they were actually enjoying their children swapping identities, it gave them a new dimension, something to explore and talk about with their friends to show how modern and enlightened they were. It was clear that as a family member who was unhappy with the situation, I was in a minority of one. There was another problem, too. I was enjoying more and more my life as a girl, not just a girl but a pretty girl. I wanted things to go back as they were, sure, but I also wanted them to stay unchanged. I couldn't have both, of course. And the girl's boarding school, the very idea of it was a nightmare. Impossible.

I helped Mom clear the table. In the kitchen, she took me to one side and spoke quietly.

"Sarah, something I want to tell you, but keep it quiet."

I nodded. "Yes, Mom?"

"You're very beautiful, you know, a pretty, lovely girl that any mother would be proud of. Sarah wasn't like that before, she was fine, but you, you're so much lovelier. I can't wait to go out and show you off to other people, I feel so proud that you're my daughter now. Isn't that wonderful?"

"Well, I guess so," I said doubtfully.

"It is, believe me," she said firmly. "Of course you have doubts, but let me help you resolve them, that's what girls are for, isn't it?"

"Yes, Mom," I said. Except that…

They had a week at home and the following morning Mom took me shopping to the mall. This time, it was her that helped me get dressed and fix my hair and makeup.

"You need to learn how to do this yourself, Missy. Sit in front of the mirror and I'll show you what to do."

Wearing only my padded bra and panties, I applied my makeup while she gave me detailed instructions. It was endless, a succession of creams, foundation, blusher, lipstick, lip gloss, mascara and eye shadow which had to be removed and re-applied when she decided that I needed to borrow her false eyelashes. When they were glued on, I had to agree my eyes looked large and glamorous. Then it was the turn of my hair, she showed me how to style it and use a range of brushes and combs, curling tongs, clips, slides and ribbons to get it looking nice. She was good at it, when we'd finished I looked better than ever with huge, dark eyes and smooth, clear skin. She helped me choose my clothes to get dressed and brought me her own waspy. "I used to wear it, honey, but you can have it now until we get you a new one, it'll hold your waist in, you need a bit more shape there."

She fitted the satin garment around me and laced it up tight, I sure knew it was there, forcing in my stomach to that breathing became something of a chore, but I did get used to it even though it was so much firmer than what I'd worn before. And it did make a difference, I could see my body looking even better, more feminine, more curvy. As

I had that thought I knew it was girl think, already I had started to alter the way I saw things, I realized. I was on a roller coaster and didn't know how to get off, or even if I wanted to get off.

Mom asked me to wear my white silk dress, the one I'd worn yesterday patterned with pale blue flowers and tied with the pale blue sash. I said I liked it too and she took it out of the closet and helped me into it.

"You'll need to put your perfume on, Missy, before you go any further."

"Ok, Mom." I squirted perfume from the bottle on my neck and wrists, a little on my 'cleavage'. Mum watched approvingly. When I'd finished I smelt as if I'd bathed in the stuff, but it seemed right and Mom liked it. Then I pulled on my pantyhose, strapped the white high heeled shoes to my feet and I was ready to go. We went downstairs and I picked up my purse. Mom put on her beige Burberry raincoat and asked me what I was going to wear to go out.

"I don't know, Mom. I wore my black raincoat when we went out last week."

She smiled. "That's not very trendy for a teenage girl. I'll find something nicer for you."

I looked at the clock, it had taken two hours to get me ready. "Mom, isn't it getting a little late now?"

"No problem, honey, we'll have lunch in town."

She went upstairs and came back with a raincoat for me

to wear, I gasped. Shiny black PVC with large white polka dots, they'd see me coming in that. When I put it on it barely reached the hem of my dress, well above the knee. She buttoned it up for me and propelled me to the mirror.

"What do you think, honey?"

It was surprisingly pretty, a kind of retro sixties mac, I'd seen a few girls wearing similar things in town so it was definitely fashionable.

"I like it, Mom, it's great."

She smiled. "I thought you would. There's a matching souwester for it somewhere around, I'll look for it later. Pick up your purse and we'll get going."

She drove us into town and I walked around, mother and daughter for the first time. She asked me to hold her arm and I put my hand in hers as we walked. We looked at a variety of different stores, all teenage girls and women's, of course. She insisted on buying me new clothes, most embarrassingly she bought five sets of gaff pants from a specialist store I didn't even know existed.

"I looked it up late last night when it became obvious you would need some special things, honey."

She had a word with the woman who managed the store and she produced a pair of breast inserts, silicone.

"You need to touch them and feel them," she said. "They feel just like the real thing, when you wear them they even warm to the temperature of your body."

I was persuaded to feel the odd things and had to agree

that they were indeed very realistic.

"Who are they for?" the woman enquired. We looked at each other, Mom and me. "They're for my daughter, of course," Mom said.

"Not this young lady here? Oh, I see. I didn't understand, I thought you really were a girl, I thought this was all for someone else."

"She is a girl," Mom said firmly.

The woman looked confused.

"Honey," Mom said. "Would you wait outside for a minute, there's something I need to sort out."

"Ok, Mom."

I went outside the store and waited across the street, it was a little too much standing outside a specialist place that sold equipment and clothes for 'medical purposes'.

Eventually Mom came out with several packages in her shopping bag. "That's done, honey, shall we go for lunch, I'm feeling hungry."

We found a chic little restaurant and she treated us to a meal. I protested at the light salad that was all she'd allow me, but she told me that pretty girls had to control their appetite as she had always had to. After a slice of ham and a few green lettuce leaves with a sliced tomato, I felt as if I hadn't eaten anything.

"It's just as well, Missy, you won't want a full stomach for where we're going."

I was mystified until she led me into a lingerie store.

"My daughter needs a full corset, something well boned with a lace up back," she said to the clerk.

"Isn't she a bit young for something old fashioned like that?" she asked.

"Do we need to go somewhere else, then?" Mom snapped at her.

The woman's expression darkened. "I'm sorry, Madam, of course not. If you'd come this way I'll show you what we have."

She led us to a rack of corsets at the back that looked horrific. I looked at Mom but she shook her head for me to keep quiet.

"Which is the firmest control?" she asked.

The clerk showed us a vicious looking garment, a long white corselette, the many bones were obvious, set into the body of the garment. It had suspender clips for stockings hanging down from the bottom of the hem.

"This is the open version, of course. Did you want open or closed?"

"She'll need both, I think, could you try her on the closed one?"

"Certainly. Miss, would you like to go into the changing room and take off your dress, I'll help you into this."

I went through the door of the changing room and managed to undo my zip and pull off my dress. The clerk came in to me.

"You'll need that waspy off to try this on, would you

like me to do it for you?"

I nodded and she unlaced it and pulled it from me. For the first time I was truly thankful for my gaff panties, without them I would almost certainly have had a problem. She put the long corset over my head and pulled it down over my hips. It fastened at the front with hooks and eyes, it didn't seem too bad, a little firmer than the waspy but not terrible, it was just so long, stiff and heavy.

"Comfortable? I'll tighten your laces."

She went behind me, told me to breathe in and pulled. And pulled, and pulled. I squirmed in pain, called out to her. "I can't breathe, it's too tight."

"That's ok, they always feel like that when you first get them on, you'll soon get used to it."

She finished tying my laces.

"Would you like me to fasten underneath the crotch for you, it's a bit fiddly when you're not used to it?"

I nodded, I still couldn't speak. The back of the corset hung down behind me, she reached through, pulled it forward and fastened it to the front with hooks and eyes.

"How's that, Miss?" she asked me.

She had a gleam in her eye, I suspected that she'd tied it so tight because of Mom speaking to her sharply.

"It's terrible," I said.

"Good, that's the way it should be," she said. "Let's show your Mom how you look."

Before I could protest, she pushed me out of the

changing room into the curtained off area at the back of the store. Mom was waiting there and looked carefully at my tightly corseted body.

"It's marvelous, honey, what a huge difference it makes. We'll take two of those and two of the open ones."

"Certainly, Madam," the clerk said and she left to find the other three my mom had ordered.

"Mom, you don't understand, I can't wear this."

"Why ever not?" she smiled.

"It's too tight, it hurts and I can hardly breathe."

"Sarah, it's a corset. Of course it's too tight, of course it hurts, you're just not used to it yet. If it wasn't too tight we'd have to find a smaller size, do you want to do that?"

"No, Mom."

"I thought not. You'd better keep it on, I'll tell the clerk and she can pack your waspy with the other corsets. Go and put your dress back on, honey."

I was compressed into a device that tortured my whole body. Every part of me was jammed into this terrible corset, even my penis and testicles, previously held discreetly inside my gaff panties had been squashed up tightly into my crotch. Is this what women had to go through to look thin, I wondered? I put my dress on and zipped it up. Mom looked over when I came out of the changing room.

"My word, I'll need to adjust your sash, honey. You've already lost several inches from your waist."

She tied my sash tighter and I glanced in the mirror, it was true, my waist was much, much smaller and my hips and bust were pushed out more prominently. I couldn't help smiling with pleasure at how good it looked, a pity it was so grueling to wear, though.

"You like it, don't you?" Mom asked me.

"Well, yeah, Mom…"

"I knew you would, honey. I'll pay for everything and we'll move on."

By the time we got into the car to go home, I was carrying four different parcels with a new dress, blouses, a skirt, underwear, pantyhose and cosmetics. And in another bag, my new corsets.

The only problem I had was going to the bathroom in the new corset, but Mom explained to me how it all worked and even came with me the first time to help me with the hooks and eyes. I was so desperate to go I even forgot to be so embarrassed. That evening I was conscious of my Dad and brother staring at my newly slim figure. For some reason, I felt proud. Hannah came to the house and helped me to go over all of my schoolwork. By the following Saturday I felt that I knew everything I needed to know about the schoolwork, it was only what I'd already done, more or less. There was one huge problem, I wasn't going and that was final. Boys didn't go to girl's schools, did they?

I told Hannah and she pointed out that I wasn't a boy,

I was a girl.

"Of course you are, Sarah, what else could you be?"

"Yeah, I know how I look, but you know what I mean."

"I think I do, but you're wrong."

At that moment, Mom came into the room. "What's up, girls?"

Hannah explained that I had cold feet about going.

"Oh, you must, honey," Mom said. "We'll be going away, and Andrew will be in New York City. You have to go to Karen Hall, besides, you'll be with Hannah. Sarah, look at me."

I looked at her determined face.

"You're only confused," she said. "I understand, but please, Sarah, it's for the best. I'd be really disappointed if you refused. Very upset, believe me, I love having you as my daughter, I feel as if I've been reborn. Bear with it, honey, you're only a little mixed up, you'll find it's for the best, really. Tell her, Hannah."

She nodded. "Your mom's right, Sarah. Besides, you're loving it really, aren't you, looking so pretty and being my best friend?"

I nodded. "Of course I'm happy you're my best friend."

"And looking pretty?"

I nodded.

"There you go then. We'll go to Karen Hall together.

CHAPTER SIX

On Sunday morning my moment of reckoning loomed closer. I felt there was only one thing I could do, I'd have to talk Mom out of it in the car on the way to Spokane. I got out of the shower and put on my underwear, my gaff, the corset which Mom laced tightly for me, afterwards I fastened the hooks and eyes under my crotch. I pulled on my thick, dark red pantyhose and Mom gave me a freshly pressed blouse to wear. When I'd buttoned it up I put on my tartan miniskirt and black shoes and checked in the mirror. I had to admit I looked like a conventional schoolgirl. We packed my two cases with everything I'd need, by the time we'd finished they were bulging. Dad came up and took them down to the hallway. I did a last minute check on my makeup, it all looked good, a little more subtle than normal, Hannah had explained that the school didn't approve of makeup, at least, visible makeup.

I went downstairs and waited.

"Where is your school raincoat, Sarah?" Mom said.

"It's packed away in the case, Mom."

"You'll need something to take with you on the journey, get your black polka dot mac and wear that."

"Ok, Mom."

I buttoned up the PVC mac, Mom came to check me out. She was holding the matching souwester that went with the raincoat. "You look lovely, honey, you can wear this as well, I'll put it on you."

She put the hat on my head and tied it under my chin. In the mirror, I looked like a refugee from the nineteen sixties, a very pretty, trendy refugee though. She gave me my purse, just then a car drew up outside.

"There's plenty of money in there as well as all of the documents you'll need for the school. I'll get Dad to take your cases out to the car."

He picked them up and carried them through the door where a car was waiting. Hannah's mom, Hannah was in the back seat, what were they doing here? Mom ushered me out to the car and said hi to Hannah and her mom, I could see Dad putting my cases in the trunk.

"We'll say goodbye then, honey, you have a wonderful time."

What? "Mom, what's this, you're not taking me?"

"No, of course not, Mrs. Blake is taking Hannah to school so she offered to take you too, there's no point in taking two cars just for two girls, is there?"

Dad came up and kissed me on the cheek. "So long, honey, work hard, enjoy yourself."

He pushed me into the car and I sat down, Mom leaned across and fastened my seat belt. Then she handed me a laptop case, it was heavy.

"That's for you, sweetie, a new laptop so you can keep in touch with us and do your homework on it, of course. Bye, girls, be good."

Mrs. Blake put the car into gear and drove off. I realized with a sinking, desperate feeling that I was on my way to a girl's boarding school.

Hannah chatted merrily all the way to Spokane.

"I love your raincoat and that dinky hat, Sarah, it's gorgeous. Did your mom get it for you?"

I nodded absently. She chatted on, talking about all of the things we'd do in school, the sports, the clubs, the girls, the clothes, it was endless. She noticed I was not speaking.

"Are you ok, Sarah? You're really quiet."

"I'm terrified," I said to her quietly. "You know why."

She nodded. "Yes, of course I do, but you shouldn't be, you know. You'll be the envy of all the other girls."

I didn't reply, I couldn't honestly work out what I wanted or didn't want, but I didn't think that this was anything to be happy about. We reached the school, a big old building, cars were arriving and dropping off lots of girls similarly dressed to Hannah and me. We reported to the lobby, where a stern faced woman checked a list and told us we were sharing a room on the first floor.

"Hurry up and get your cases unpacked, girls, dinner will be served at six o'clock."

We struggled up the stairs through hordes of schoolgirls and found our way to our room. We went in, slammed the door shut and threw the cases on our beds. I looked around, it wasn't too bad, a bed, closet and chest for each of us as well as a desk and chair. There was a door to an attached bathroom, which gave me considerable relief. We unpacked our cases, hung everything in the closets that needed to be hung up, put the rest away in the drawers and I set up my new laptop on my desk.

"What do you think?" Hannah asked me.

I shook my head. "I don't know, Hannah, it terrifies me."

She took my head in her hands and stared at me from close up. "Sarah, you're a pretty girl, there's nothing to be worried about. Besides, I'll always be with you, so chill out and let's enjoy it."

"Ok, I'll try," I said.

"I like your new laptop, that was really generous of your mom."

"You can use it too, if you want."

She smiled. "Thanks Sarah."

She saw my woebegone face. "Oh, come on, I'll show

you around the school, let's explore."

We spent an hour looking over my new school, I'd never seen so many girls in one place before, they were everywhere. No, we were everywhere, I reminded myself. We went back to our room and got ready for dinner. When I'd touched up my makeup, I saw that Hannah was wearing her school blazer.

"You'll need to wear yours too, it's the school rule."

I dug it out of the closet and put it on, and then we went to the dining hall and sat down to eat. Two of Hannah's friends sat with us, Emily Roberts and Amanda Wu, who looked to be half Asian oriental.

As we ate, Emily looked at my hair.

"Your hair is nice in that style, Sarah, but have you thought of putting it up in bunches, you know, the kind that stand out at the sides? You can fasten them with pretty bows and ribbons and they look terrific."

I felt grateful to be included in their conversation, even to have been noticed as a girl.

"Yeah, she's right, Sarah, it would look good, I'll help you do it if you like," Hannah said.

"Thanks, I'd like that."

We spent the rest of the evening in the common room chatting about what we'd been up to during the summer break. I just sat and listened, it seemed to me that all I had done was to be suckered into this moment. Finally we went back to our room to prepare for bed.

"Sarah, your mom said you'd be a bit embarrassed about this bit and she asked me to help you. Let me unlace your corset for you so that you don't need to worry. She told me everything, so don't think there's going to be any kind of a problem, ok?"

I nodded and took off my blouse, skirt, shoes and pantyhose. She went behind my back and untied my corset and loosened the laces.

"Have you taken you pills?" she asked me.

"Shit, no, I forgot."

"Yeah, your mom thought you might. You do need to take them, you know, it's important if you're going to be a girl."

"I know that, the last thing I want is hair growing all over me."

She looked at me curiously. "I guess there is that, too. Sarah, so that there's nothing between us, no issues, let me see how your crotch looks in those panties."

I stood still while she looked. "They do a damn good job, if I didn't know better, I'd think you were all girl in there. Your tits are coming on nicely too."

I looked down. To my surprise and horror, I had two small girl's breasts where before it had been reasonably flat.

"Jesus Christ, how did that happen?"

"Lucky it did, at least you look feminine. Think what would happen if someone saw you with a boy's chest," she grinned.

"I guess so, but why has it happened?"

"Don't you know? You'd better talk to your mom."

"Yeah, I will."

She saw me looking forlorn again. "Hey, Sarah, cheer up, they're a nice pair of breasts, quite pretty. Nothing for a girl to worry about, you should be proud."

"Yes, but…"

"No buts," she said adamantly. "You are a girl, just remember it. Have you got that?"

I nodded.

"Good. Put your nightie on and get into bed, we'll have a long day tomorrow."

When I had my new nightie on, floral design, pale pastels, in a pretty pattern with matching panties, she kissed me goodnight.

"You're going to be fine you know, together we'll get along great."

Then she kissed me firmly on the lips. "Really great."

I looked at her horrified. "Hannah, don't forget I'm a girl!"

She laughed. "Now you're getting it. Of course you're a girl, and this is a girl's school. What do you think we do in a place like with without any boys?"

Our alarm clock woke us early, I showered, took my pills and Hannah helped in into my corset. I picked up my miniskirt but she stopped me.

"No, not today, girly. This is a Monday, a school day, you need to wear a gymslip and blouse, those are the rules. You'll need the school tie attached to the blouse, it's a little thing that clips under the front of the collar."

I put the skirt back in the closet and got out my gymslip and put it on, tied the belt, fastened my tie like an inverted V to my blouse. I checked my face in the mirror, it seemed ok.

"What about the bunches that Emily suggested, we've got plenty of time, do you want me to do them for you?"

I hesitated, but only for a moment. Ten minutes later, my hair stood out either side in modern looking bunches, tied with regulation colored ribbons. We picked up our bags and went down to begin.

I blended in with all of the other girls, all dressed like me in gymslips and white blouses. In the long corridor was an enormous mirror, I checked my image and was amused to see the way I looked, a trendy young schoolgirl with bunches sticking out from my hair. Hannah knew the way of course and we went straight to the classroom for the first lesson which was American history. The teacher, Miss Bainbridge, noticed me straight away.

"You're new, aren't you?"

"Yes, Miss. I'm Sarah Hague"

"Have you been to registration with the deputy headmistress?"

I said I hadn't.

"Very well, make sure you do so today, welcome to Karen Hall Academy for Girls, Sarah."

The lesson was a breeze, nothing I couldn't handle. During the break I went to the deputy headmistress and she talked to me for a few minutes about observing school rules.

"Are you wearing makeup, Sarah?"

I thought about it for a moment, but she was no fool, lying to her could be a big mistake.

"Just a little, Mrs. Bush."

"We don't allow it in school, Sarah. Get rid of it when you have time later today. But welcome to Karen Hall Academy for Girls, I'm sure you're going to be very happy here."

She handed me a book of school rules and I left her office.

We shared a table for lunch with Emily and Amanda, they admired my bunches. By the afternoon I'd survived a maths lesson and a geography lesson and was exhausted. The pace was hard, even though I'd done much of the work before. The school was determined to set a very high standard and at the end of the day I had enough homework to keep me busy for a week. Hannah was unsympathetic.

"That's the way it is here, Sarah, I've been doing it for a year already. You'll get used to it, don't worry."

"What have we got tomorrow?" I asked her.

She checked the schedule. "It looks like games, I guess

we'll be playing netball. Have you got your kit?"

I nodded. "Yeah, Mom packed all of that for me."

"Have you ever played netball before?"

It dawned on me then that I had a problem, a serious problem. I knew as much about netball as I did about the dark side of the moon.

"God, no, I haven't. How can I handle this, a game that every girl in America learns as soon as she starts school and I've never even played it?"

"I think I'd better go over the rules with you, Sarah. It's not too hard, don't worry about it."

She set up a small practice area in the room and went through the game with me. It was sort of like basketball, except that you couldn't run with the ball.

"That's stupid," I said.

"You'd better tell the netball coach, then," Hannah laughed. "I'm sure she'd love to hear that."

After an hour I was sure that I had a grasp of the game. Hannah was concerned about me playing in my heavy corset.

"Do you think you'll be able to move around the court, or should you take it off tomorrow?"

I thought about it. But the corset was becoming part of me, still a little uncomfortable, though not painful, but it was a garment that more than anything gave me my feminine figure.

"I'll be ok, I'll wear it."

CHAPTER SEVEN

After lunch the next day we went back to our room and changed into our short, pleated netball skirts and polo tops with the school emblem. Luckily I was drawn on Hannah's team and I put on the tabard that the coach gave me. Out on the court, I stayed in the background, terrified to draw attention to myself as a total beginner. I barely managed to stop myself running and dribbling with the ball when it came to me, I doubt that anything would have given everything away more than that. But I threw the ball to another girl who scored and we all cheered madly. Was this really me, I wondered, pleated netball skirt, cheering another girl on a netball court when she scored? I shook my head with disbelief. Afterwards when we were walking back, Hannah asked me if I'd enjoyed myself. Before I could even think about it, I told her it was great, I'd had a brilliant time.

"So you like the school?"

"Yeah, it's great, Hannah, I love it."

I looked across at her, she had a sly smile on her face. I realized what I'd said.

The following afternoon we had the first of our makeup and grooming for young ladies lesson. We had to change into our miniskirts and blouses and sit in rows while a teacher showed us elements of makeup theory. It was a whole new area for me and I watched and listened, fascinated by the lengths girls like me had to go to to make ourselves look pretty. Then we sat and applied a range of foundation creams, blushers, eye makeup, lipstick and glosses. Afterwards, we went to the cafeteria with Emily and Amanda. All four of us looked glossy and glamorous after the makeup lesson, although we would have to remove it all before long. When school ended, we went to our room to start on our homework. Hannah had been slightly strained that day, I asked her why.

"Sarah, don't you feel it, the pull between us?"

"I don't understand," I replied.

She burst into tears and I held her to my breasts. Christ, breasts! I felt her pushing into them, they were tender, soft, and slightly spongy. They were definitely growing each day, was that good or bad?

"When we kissed, Sarah, I felt so warm towards you, didn't you feel anything towards me?"

"Well, yeah, I did, of course I did."

"Thank goodness," she continued. "I thought it was just me. Kiss me, Sarah, show me how you feel."

Without thinking, I pulled her face towards mine and kissed her. I felt her tongue press into my mouth and start exploring inside, I put my own tongue in her mouth and we were both holding each other tightly, the passion between us fierce and vibrant.

"Sarah, would you do something for me?" she asked.

"Yes, of course. What do you want me to do?"

I thought she'd ask me to make love to her, which for some reason didn't arouse me at all like it would have done once. My cock, held tightly inside the gaff and the stiff material of my corset didn't even respond, it was like I'd taken tranquilizers. I told her the problem, it worried me somewhat.

"Of course it won't react," she smiled. "The tablets you take to stop hair growth will have that effect. No, I want you to use this on me."

She took a small case out of her drawer and showed me her dildo, a large, flesh colored rubber cock. My eyes widened in surprise.

"You want me to use that on you?"

"Of course. You're a girl now, silly, it's what we girls do. You'll have to undress me, darling."

Darling? Well, if I was doing this, I guess it was ok to call me darling. I pulled off her miniskirt and unbuttoned her blouse, slowly and tenderly.

"Did you worry that you'd still have a normal male desire while you were here?" she asked me.

"Well, I wasn't sure, but yeah, I guess it did concern me a bit."

She grinned. "There's no fear of that, believe me. The high doses you take mean that your hormones are largely female now, that's why your mom was so careful to make sure that I reminded you to take them. Sarah, listen to what I'm saying. I know you have doubts and worries, but you are a girl. Just enjoy it, you are having fun, aren't you, you said you were?"

"I am, it's true. It's just, strange."

"Soon you'll forget that anything was ever any different. Now come on, girly, screw me, give me a good one."

I pulled off her pantyhose and panties, then unfastened her bra. She lay before me, beautiful, smooth, and aroused beyond belief. I touched her cunt and it was already wet, soaking wet. I gently rubbed her clit and she arched her back, groaning in ecstasy. Then I slid it in and she almost screamed in pleasure.

"Hey, keep it down, Hannah, they'll hear you back in Portland."

She giggled. "I couldn't care less, this is heaven. Rub my clit again, please, that was wonderful."

I stroked her glorious clit and was happy to see her writhing in the throes of exquisite pleasure. I got the dildo working in and out to a decent rhythm and stroked her clit at the same time. When I bent over to lightly kiss her tits she almost had an instant orgasm. I kept up the pressure on her vagina, the dildo and clitoral stroking rendering her almost totally incapable.

"Kiss me, Sarah, please, I need you so much."

I bent down and moved my body totally around so that I was kneeling behind her, my face was over hers and my arms stretched down to her crotch. I kissed her, gently, making it last, feeling the heat that burned out of her. Our tongues collided, touched and carried on exploring, hot, wet and so, so tactile. It was almost as if we could understand each other just by the touch of our tongues alone. Then she came, a huge, surging wave of passion that swept over her and lifted part of her body off the bed, she sobbed, panted, groaned, it was all I could do to contain the worst of it by kissing her again. She lay back, totally sated.

A few moments later, she opened her eyes.

"That was wonderful, my darling. How can I give something back to you?"

I shook my head. "I honestly don't know, nothing seems to be working down there."

"Maybe you'll get it sorted out eventually," she said.

I didn't understand. "How would I do that?"

"You know, Sarah, surgery, they could create a beautiful vagina down there. Then I could use the dildo on you."

My brain spun away into a gaping, black hole of despair.

"You can't be serious, how could you even suggest such a thing?"

"But surely, Sarah, you can't carry on as a girl with a penis, can you? You'll have to have it done eventually. You're getting a gorgeous pair of tits, you just need the other bit sorted out now."

I sat on the floor and my mind felt tortured. Surgery, a sex change, it was an enormous and insane suggestion and I told her. She looked disappointed.

"So you want to go back to being a guy, is that what you're saying?"

"No, of course I don't, I love being what I am, a girl."

As I said it, I realized it was true. It had happened so quickly, in a matter of weeks, from a silly game to me becoming a girl attending a girl's boarding school. And just as quickly, I had become totally comfortable with the girl that I had become. Almost.

"You've got a lot to think about," she said.

"Let's get ready for bed,"

"It's a bit early, isn't it?"

"Can we just do it, darling?"

Her voice had a strange tone to it but I ignored it, we removed the makeup from that afternoon's lesson and Hannah unlaced my corset and helped me take it off.

"Why not wear your waspy in bed, Sarah, it will keep your body in the right shape and the corset will be much more comfortable during the day. It must be hard being placed into this awful thing all day long."

"It is," I admitted. "Ok, I'll try it."

She helped me fasten myself into the waspy and laced it for me. It was tight, but not uncomfortable and I felt quite sexy wearing it. My gaff panties were split in the rear, so that I could go to the bathroom, Hannah put cream on her fingers and pushed them into my hole. It was heaven. Then she used her other hand to gently brush my tits and I jerked as if I'd been hit with an electric shock.

"Lie on your side, my darling, let me give you a little pleasure."

I rolled to my side and she kept her fingers inside my ass. Her hand came back and played with my nipples but her fingers suddenly withdrew from inside my anus. I felt a sense of loss, they'd given me a warm feeling of pleasure, but then I felt a hard object pushed into me, further and further.

"Christ, I can't take all of this, it's huge," I told her.

"Of course you can," she replied. "We've all done it."

She moved around so that this time it was her that was kneeling at my head, one hand moving the dildo gently in my butt, the other stroking my tits. She bent her head down and kissed me and I felt wave after wave of pleasure and arousal shooting through me. I couldn't have an orgasm, the pills had put paid to that possibility and my cock was just a useless appendage trapped between my legs. But the arousal came from my ass, from my prostate gland that Hannah was massaging with the dildo and from my tits that she was expertly stroking. Something happened, something strange, I felt a hot warmth shooting through me, an intense, agonized ecstasy that I'd never felt before. I writhed and moaned with pleasure, then it eased off and I lay still.

"My darling, if I didn't know better I'd say you just had a female orgasm," Hannah grinned.

I shook my head. "I don't know, but whatever it was, it was pretty amazing."

"Welcome to the female sex, my darling Sarah."

By Friday evening, I'd fully settled into the life of a schoolgirl at Karen Hall Academy for Girls. I learned the intricacies of netball, became increasingly expert at makeup and deportment and worked hard at my lessons. During the nights, Hannah and I shared a bed and made love as often as we could. At dinner that evening the other girls received welcome news, for me it was a nasty shock. Miss Charlotte Wilson, our headmistress, stood up in the dining hall and made an announcement.

"Girls, we are holding a school dance here in the dining hall tomorrow evening. All girls are required to attend and we have invited boys from the local senior high school to come and partner you. You may wear your best dresses and use makeup, so I want to see a really good turnout."

I turned to Hannah. "What's this, a dance with boys? I can't do that."

Emily and Amanda looked on puzzled. "Why on earth not, Sarah?" Amanda said. "It's great to have some boys coming here, I'm fed up with seeing only girls all week."

"Besides," Emily added. "You're one of the prettiest girls in the school, what have you got to worry about, they'll be flocking all over you."

That's what I'm afraid of, I wanted to tell them. But I said that I was just a bit down about a couple of things.

"You shouldn't be, Sarah, you're a real babe, you've got everything going for you," Emily said to me.

On Saturday afternoon we started preparing for the evening. After I'd showered Hannah laced me ruthlessly into my corset, tighter than ever. When I protested she just said to wait until I was in my dress and see the difference, then I wouldn't complain about it. I put on my pantyhose and sat to fix my makeup and nails. When I was done, Hannah helped to pile my hair high on top of my head in a glamorous, formal style, it was held in place with a huge, silver, jeweled hair slide. I put on my lovely pink, patterned dress and tightened the wide black patent belt. The last time I'd worn it I hadn't had my heavy corset on, now I was amazed to see the belt fasten five inches tighter than before.

"I told you," my friend said. "Look in the mirror."

I had to hand it to her I looked very, very slim, graceful and elegant.

"Well, princess?"

"Thanks," I said. "You were right."

I found a small, black patent evening purse that Mom had packed for me and transferred my things to it. Then I sat down again to put on my jewelry, earrings, necklace, bracelets and cocktail watch.

We stood side by side to look at each other in the mirror, Hannah was stunning too, wearing a little black dress, above the knee length and her hair in little ringlets that fell to her shoulders. She had high heeled shoes, like mine they were black patent with five inch heels.

"You don't think we look like a pair of hookers?" I asked her.

She grinned. "I hope so."

Then she saw my jaw drop open with worry. "I'm only joking, we look great."

We went down the wide staircase side by side, arm in arm and into the hall where the dance was being held. It was decorated with bunting, colored lights and tables set out all along each side. A group of guys were leaning against the soft drinks bar, as they saw us enter the room they did a double take and I smiled inside.

"Tell me you're not happy," Hannah said."

"I can't, I feel great. Hannah, the guys are all looking at us, what do we do?"

"Fuck 'em," she said. "We'll decide who we talk to and dance with, not them. I guess you don't know how to give the gentle brush off, do you?"

I shook my head. "I'll show you when they come up to us," she said. "But what is more important is how to do the gentle come on. That's the really serious part."

CHAPTER EIGHT

We were standing in a group drinking cokes, Hannah, Emile, Amanda and me. It didn't take long before the music started, we only had to wait for a DJ on the stage to talk far too much like they always seemed to. A good looking jock came up to our group and zeroed in on me.

"How about it, babe, you going to dance with me?"

I looked at Hannah and shook my head, a tiny movement that only she would have noticed. She looked at her watch. "Don't forget that Alan, your boyfriend is due to arrive in a minute, Sarah, he's been training at the gym all day, lifting weights and pumping iron, he wouldn't be too happy."

I looked at the guy and shrugged, he walked away in disgust. The evening went on in the same vein, until late the only person I danced with was Hannah. Towards the end, though, I allowed myself to be persuaded to dance with another good looking guy, he seemed quite nice until he put his hands on my tits. I threw them off and got rid of him when the song finished. We went back to our room and I stripped Hannah off and hungrily made love to her, this time I used my mouth to bring her to the edge of orgasm, then plunged the dildo into her dripping wet fanny and played it in and out, my other hand massaging her clit to bring her to a climax. She wanted to return the favor, but I was very tired after the experience of my new school and my new life, so I went to bed on my own.

In truth, I'd been rocked by the episode with the guys at the dance. Although I'd only danced with one, we had talked with several of them and they seemed like decent guys. If I was honest with myself, I fancied a couple of them, not in a queer way, but as a girl. It was very worrying, I'd have to talk to someone about it, but who? The pills, which I now understood to be female hormones, had taken away my male sex drive completely, which was a good thing in a girl's school. The trouble was they had replaced it with a strong female sex drive, one that I was unable to fully indulge in. I had Hannah to talk to, though, my best friend who was wonderful and she was obviously totally in love with me. The difficulty was that she obviously loved me as a girl, not as a boy. It was quite obvious that if I ever did go back to my old, male self, she'd lose all interest. Was she a lesbian, was it that simple? No probably not, I suspected she was bisexual.

But she only wanted the female me, not the male version. Did I love her, I wondered? After I thought about it for a few seconds, I realized that I loved her deeply, she was so pretty, so perfect that I wanted us to always be together. But as what? And me, what did I want for myself? I totally enjoyed being a pretty girl, pampered, loved, looked after, pretty clothes and a first rate school. Did I want to go back to being a boy? The thought made me shudder, having to give up wearing my beautiful dresses and making up my face, putting my hair in a variety of attractive styles. I wanted to look sexy, yeah, admit it to yourself, Sarah, I wanted to look like a sexy girl. And I did look like a sexy girl, all I had to do was to stay as I was. But what of the future? It could only have one end, I knew that. I couldn't stay half girl, half boy. I had to choose.

On Sunday morning I got out of bed, showered and took my pills. Hannah helped lace me into my corset and I put on my blouse and tartan miniskirt. I told her I wanted to go for walk on my own to think things through.

"Are we ok, Sarah, there's not a problem is there?"

"Hannah, you're the one thing I don't need to think through," I told her, giving her a kiss. She smiled and helped me do my hair into bunches as I made up my face. It was Sunday so I made a more thorough job of it, the works, foundation, lipstick blusher, eye shadow, mascara, I even used my eyebrow pencil to touch up around my eyes.

"You look lovely, princess," she said to me. "You'd

better wear a coat, the weather is not very good."

I peeped out of the window, it was raining lightly so I buttoned myself into my short, shiny black mac with the white polka dots and put on the souwester, tying it under my chin.

"Take care now," she said as I walked out of the room.

I went out of the front door and walked towards the main gate, thinking a stroll around the area might clear my head. A car came through the gate and stopped next to me.

"Excuse me, Miss, we're looking for the main entrance, is it straight ahead?"

I nodded and pointed and was about to walk on when I recognized Ellen, in the driving seat was Andrew.

They were as astonished as I was to see them.

"Sarah, how are things going?" Andrew asked me.

I said they were fine. Ellen smirked at me in my girly mac and souwester. "Gosh, you look pretty, Sarah."

"Sis, let's go into town and find somewhere for coffee, we came to see you. Jump in the back."

I climbed in the back of the car and he drove away to find a diner. It was quiet on the Sunday morning so we parked on the main street and went into a coffee bar. I removed my hat, unbuttoned my mac and sat down, Ellen looked at my schoolgirl uniform smiled. "Yes, you look very pretty, how are you getting on?"

"I'm fine, it's ok," I said, not wanting to rise to her bait.

I did ask her where Adam, her boyfriend was.

"We broke up, it didn't work out."

"I'm sorry," I said.

"I'm not, I'm glad it's finished. Besides, I've got Andrew now."

So that was the way it was. She was a lesbian. But what about Andrew, Jesus Christ, it was as complicated a situation as my own? I asked them how things were at Columbia.

"It's great, Sis," Andrew said. "Ellen and I found a small apartment in the Village, New York City is really wild, parties, clubs, theatre, it's a twenty four hour a day city, never sleeps. Tell us, what do you get up to here?"

So I told them about my netball games, the makeup and deportment lessons, English, maths and geography.

"So, what do you do in the evenings?" Andrew asked.

"I'm always busy, most of the evening is taken up with homework."

There was a silence that hung there for almost a minute.

"Well that sounds great," Ellen said abruptly. I looked at her sharply. "I like it, Ellen."

They were open mouthed. "You really like it?" Andrew asked.

"Sure I do, it's not bright lights and big city like you've got, but school life here is cool, I've made some good friends and it's enjoyable, most of the time anyway."

"To be honest, Sis, that's what I wanted to talk to you

about. I don't ever want things to go back the way they were, I want it to stay permanent. Ellen and I have made plans and we want to be a normal couple."

I was puzzled. "So go ahead. What difference does it make to me?"

He took a deep breath. "It makes a big difference. We want to get married after we graduate and that means using my documents, birth certificate and so on."

"So?" I was still puzzled.

Ellen interrupted. "Which would mean that you would have to keep your documents. For life."

Then I understood. "So there would be no going back, ever?"

They shook their heads. "No, Sis, there wouldn't," Andrew said. "It would mean us putting it on a formal, legal basis. Mom and Dad know all about it, I've been in touch with them by email."

"So it's up to me then?"

They looked at me, two pairs of eyes staring at me intently. "Yes, it's up to you."

I sat quietly for a few minutes, thinking, or trying to think, but my mind was a blank.

"I need time to think about it," I said.

"We have to know today, Sis."

"Ok, take me back to school, I'll meet you after lunch and we'll talk about it some more."

I buttoned up my mac and tied my souwester under my

chin. As we walked out of the diner I saw a pretty girl in a polka dot mac with another girl who looked quite plain and boring. You can smirk, Ellen but I like the way I look.

They took me back to the school gate and agreed to pick me up in the same place a three o'clock. I went in and walked up the drive.

"You, girl," a voice called over to me, a frosty faced woman. A teacher, obviously.

"Yes, Miss?"

"Why are you wearing that coat in school, don't you know the rules?"

I told her I didn't know I was doing anything wrong.

"It's quite simple," she said. "On school premises you wear school uniform at all times. Do you have your uniform raincoat here?"

"Yes, I do, it's in my room."

"Very well, wear it if you need a coat to go out, not that fashion item. This is not a disco, you know." She stalked away, I was relieved to have got off so lightly

I went up to our room where I found Hannah who was studying furiously, making notes on a pad.

"I need to talk to you, I've got a big decision to make," I said to her.

She looked up and smiled. "Ok, shoot."

I told her about meeting Andrew and Ellen and what they wanted from me. She couldn't see the problem either, just as I hadn't, so I explained further.

"Yeah, I understood the first time," she said. "The swap stays permanent. But I still don't see the problem. What did you say to them?"

I told her that I was meeting them this afternoon.

"Can I come with you, Sarah?"

"Of course you can, but the real dilemma is, what do I do? I honestly don't know."

"I think you do know," my best friend said. She took me by the shoulders and held my face close to hers. "You know what life is like for you now and you know what life was like before. Were you really happy before? Do you want what you had, you should remember that all of the happiness you have now would be gone? Or do you want to keep what you've got now? And keep me, of course."

I knew the answer, but I explained that it had all started in such a silly way and I never intended for it to get this far.

"I know," she smiled. "I was there, remember, when they said how pretty you looked as Sarah, I couldn't believe it at the time. But they were right, Sarah, you're a girly, why don't you accept it?"

I still hadn't decided, or maybe I'd decided but couldn't bring myself to admit the enormity of it all. We went to the dining room for lunch. I was quiet all through the meal, Emily and Amanda chattered happily, Hannah kept quiet and let me think it all through, or try to anyway. Afterwards we went up to our room to get ready to go and meet Andrew and Ellen. I told her about the teacher who had told me to wear my school raincoat. She smiled.

"Yeah, some of them are old dragons, but I suppose we'd better play ball. It's cold outside, is it?"

I nodded and we got our navy blue raincoats out of our closets and buttoned ourselves into them. We checked that the hoods were folded neatly on each of us and went down the stairs and out through the main door. As we walked along the drive, arm in arm, she looked at me, her eyebrows raised. I shook my head.

"I just don't know. I'll decide when the moment comes."

David and Ellen were in the car at the end of the school drive, watching us walking towards them. They were both smiling, Ellen in fact wore a smile that was once more suspiciously like a smirk. I knew what they saw, two schoolgirl friends in their uniform raincoats walking arm in arm, just like lots of other girls who were walking in the grounds. We reached the car.

"That's really sweet," Ellen said.

Andrew told her to knock it off. "You two girls get in the back seat and we'll find somewhere for coffee."

We drove into town and found a diner with a deserted booth in the far corner. The waitress arrived, smiled at Hannah and me, recognizing girls from the local school and took our order for coffee. We waited in silence until she had brought them and went away. Eventually, Andrew broke impasse.

"Have you thought about it, Sis? Do you have an

answer?"

"What would happen if I said yes?"

"In that case, I'd get the documents drawn up in the week and come back here next weekend for you to sign."

"And the alternative?" I asked.

He looked haunted. "I honestly don't know, Sis. I guess we'd have to think about that one. Maybe I could email Mom and Dad, by the way, they're back in the US on Friday so they'll probably come here to visit you."

"Would you definitely fix up for them to visit? I do want to see them."

"Yeah, of course, I know they'd love to come."

"I'll sign the forms, then. Provided they're both there when I do. And Hannah, of course."

I felt my friend take hold of my hand and grip it tightly. Andrew visibly relaxed, as did Ellen.

"That's wonderful, Sis, I'll get the papers drawn up in the week. You won't regret this, you know. What are you going to do now?"

"Go back to school and get on with my homework, I guess."

He laughed. "No, I meant in the long term, what are you going to do with your life? Your new life, I mean."

"I'm not sure, Hannah wants to get to Wellesley and I intend to apply too."

We looked at each other, the atmosphere was slightly uncomfortable. I could see that Ellen was smirking again and I couldn't resist the urge to lash out.

"You think you've won, don't you? Both of you. But you haven't. However this all started off, I'm enjoying a lifestyle now that I love, great friends, a great school and lots to look forward to, before my life was just miserable. And there's one other thing, Ellen. You'll never be as pretty as me, ever, will you?"

She opened her mouth in surprise, I could see that I'd hit the mark. Hannah held onto my hand tightly.

"Could you take us back to school, me and my friend have got homework to catch up on."

CHAPTER NINE

We worked on our homework all evening and when we went to bed, it was a shared bed.

"You know how happy I am," my friend said as we held each other.

"Me too," I replied. "Do you want me to use your dildo on you?"

"I thought you'd never ask, go on, fuck me, I feel really horny this evening."

So I did, I'd been stroking her clit for a while and it was already soaking wet as arousal took over her whole body. I was only wearing my gaff panties, otherwise I was naked, as was Hannah. While I lay beside her using both hands on the dildo and her clit, she was stroking my tits, the feeling was tremendous.

"Are you going to up the hormone dose now that you've decided?" she asked.

I hadn't thought about it.

"They'll develop much better if you do," she added. "Besides, you'll progress much quicker towards everything else, you'll feel much more female."

"I already do feel female," I laughed.

"Then you'll feel even more so," she said.

"In that case I'll up the dose," I replied.

We were quiet as I stoked her arousal, then she came, slowly at first and then groaning to a huge orgasm, her body nearly hit the ceiling.

"You want me to screw you too, Sarah?"

"I do," I replied. "But first I want you to just stroke my tits for a while, it's a nice feeling."

"I know that," she smiled.

She kissed each of my tits and carried on stroking them. After half an hour of gentle bliss, she pushed the dildo into my rear and fucked me, kneeling over my head so that she could kiss me and keep stroking my tits with her free hand. When she finished, I'd had a warm, glowing feeling of pleasure, not quite an orgasm, I knew, but it would do for now.

"Are you frightened of the surgery, darling."

I nodded. "Yeah, I guess I am, but I haven't got any choice. At the moment I'm not one gender or the other."

"That's not true," she said hotly. "Just because you started off wrong doesn't mean you're any less of a girl. You said you were unhappy, did you never guess why it was?"

I thought back to my childhood, to seeing girls in pretty dresses and thinking how nice they would look on me. At the relentless pressure to be so macho, to conform and be something I hated when all I wanted was to do the gentler things in life, to be like all the other...Yes, like the other girls.

"I didn't realize, but subconsciously I'm certain I knew, I just couldn't put it into words."

She grinned. "Tell you what, princess, let's celebrate. We'll go into town next Friday, there's a band playing at a club and we can let our hair down. We'll wear our pretty dresses and be the envy of the other girls. We can pull a couple of boys, too."

I shook my head. "I don't want to pull a boy, Hannah."

"I know you don't, but you must. Every girl flirts with boys, it's part of what we are, you'll have to get used to it, girly."

On the Friday evening, we got ready to go out. I took extra trouble with my makeup and hair. I wore my purple dress that Mom had bought me and tied the sash, pleased that it was so tight over my tiny waist. Hannah used her curling tongs to put my hair in ringlets and fastened my large jeweled slide into it. I painted my nails and glued on false eyelashes, my friend said that I needed to go all the way and make myself irresistible. I put on my high heels and took a look in the mirror, a glossy, beautiful girl stared back at me. It was time to go.

"You'll need a coat," she said. "What have you got?"

"Only my mac and my school raincoat," I said miserably. "I left the black coat at home, for some reason."

"You can't wear your school raincoat," she said with a grin. "It'll have to be the mac, but it does look pretty, so you'll be fine."

I buttoned myself into my short polka dot mac and looked at Hannah. She was radiant, pretty and happy in the little black dress she'd decided to wear tonight. She put on her coat, a short black trench like the one my Mom had lent me and we went out.

At first the dance was a nightmare, there were plenty of other girls from our school and plenty of boys looking for dates and we had to fend the boys off in droves, it was so tiring. In the end we wound up with two good looking local boys and we drank and danced with them for most of the evening. My boyfriend Peter, towered over me, he was well over six feet tall. He told me about his life in the town of Spokane, where he was a senior high pupil at the local school. He was planning to become a software engineer and talked enthusiastically about his future plans. He asked me about my own life and I told him most of it, only omitting certain details that were a part of my old life. When he bent his head towards me and pulled my lips towards him to kiss me I let him do it and realized for the first time what it felt like being female, how much the hormones had altered my psyche so that I was, save for my embarrassing genitalia, no longer a guy but almost completely female. After the dance he asked to see me again but I managed to turn him down gently.

On Sunday Andrew and Ellen turned up for me and Hannah they drove back home to Portland. Because we were going away for the day we'd dressed in our pretty dresses, I wore the white floral dress with a tight patent leather belt, Hannah had plaited my hair and I had a pretty slide in the top. On my feet I wore my white high heeled strappy shoes, my makeup was perfect and I felt that I was dressed for the occasion. The weather was warm and we walked to the gate together, I had my mac under my arm with the souwester tucked into the pocket. When Andrew and Ellen arrived they saw two beautiful girls in pretty dresses waiting for them. I wasn't sure, but I was certain I saw a gleam of envy from the rather plainer looking Ellen. We rode home in the back of the car and arrived at our home. Mom and Dad came out to greet me, they were ecstatic when they saw me.

"I'm so happy, Sarah, you're so beautiful I can hardly believe you're mine," Mom said.

Dad gave me a kiss on the cheek, smiled and we went inside the house.

There was a stranger sitting in our lounge and he was introduced as the family lawyer. He'd drawn up the agreements and asked for a quiet moment to talk to me about them. We went into the dining room and closed the door.

"You realize young lady that this is binding and permanent?"

I nodded and he shook his head.

"I can't really believe what I'm seeing. Is it true that you were once a boy, Andrew, and your brother Andrew was once a girl?"

"Yes, it is. All true."

"Well, well, all I can say is that if you were ever a boy it was a big mistake, you truly are a very attractive girl. Obviously being a boy was a mistake, your parents are putting it all right, paying for the surgery and so on. That's written down in the agreement, they're investing a lot of money to put things as they should be. Would you like to read through it all?"

I shook my head. "No, not really, I trust Mom and Dad to do it properly."

"Ok, well let's go and sign it all."

We got up and went back into the lounge.

"Mr. and Mrs. Hague, it's all agreed, we just need to sign and witness the documents."

He laid them out on the table and pointed to where I had to sign, they were witnessed by Ellen, Andrew and me were handed several signed copies. He shook my hand. "Congratulations, you are now fully and legally Miss Sarah Hague."

Andrew went through a similar signing process and the lawyer left. Andrew and Ellen left too, they had a long way to go back to New York City. We agreed to stay for a while and Mom asked me to walk with her so that she had a chance to talk to me, Hannah stayed to chat to my dad. We went to the door and it was pouring with rain outside. I put on my mac and tied the souwester under my chin. Mom looked down at my strappy high heels.

"You can't go out in those, Sarah, your feet will get soaking wet and you'll ruin the shoes. I've got some boots I bought to go with the mac, you can borrow them."

I took off my heels and she produced a pair of knee high shiny rubber boots. I pulled them on and checked out my appearance in the mirror.

"Mom, I can't wear these, I look like a schoolgirl."

She looked at me, puzzled. Then it hit me and I laughed. Of course I looked like a schoolgirl.

While we walked, Mom talked to me about the arrangements she'd made for surgery at the local hospital. "You must be looking forward to getting it over with and putting it all behind you."

I nodded. "That's true, Mom, I am. It's a bit frightening, of course, but there's not really a choice, is there?"

"No, there isn't," she said. "Especially now, it has to be done. I'll see if I can expedite it at all for you."

We walked on and she talked about guys and girls, clothes, makeup, underwear, even emotions.

"I guess the pills have made your emotions pretty much female," she said. "Have you kissed a boy yet?"

I reddened and she laughed. "I see you have. Why shouldn't you, it's quite normal when you're a girl? What about college, you need to get some applications in, I know that you don't want to go to Columbia?"

"Hannah wants to go to Wellesley, if she's accepted, I'd like to go with her. She's my best friend."

"No half measure for you, young lady then. Do you think you'll get the grades?"

"I think so, Mom, we're working hard, every evening and most weekends too."

"Let's hope so then."

Mom took us back to school and we continued to work hard. Our grades were excellent and we kept up the pressure to get to our chosen college. When it came to the end of the trimester, Hannah was going to Florida with her family for Christmas celebrations and I went home. We had a long break, nearly four weeks and I planned to relax and recharge my batteries ready for the New Year. On the way home, Mom surprised me by telling me she'd fixed an interview with a local consultant. I was daydreaming and missed what she was saying.

"Why would I want to see a consultant, Mom, he'll know I'm not completely female, won't he?"

She smiled. "That's why you're seeing him, he's going to discuss with you the arrangements for surgery. As you've been taking hormones for so long, the process is much quicker and easier. How are your breasts coming along, by the way, what do they measure now?"

For a moment I was embarrassed, but that was old thinking, I was my mother's daughter and it was quite normal for her to ask.

"I think they're about a thirty eight B, Mom."

"Hmm, that's not bad. Would you like them to be bigger?"

"Well, a C would be nice, sure, they haven't got much shape at the moment."

"I'm sure they'll get there, honey."

At home I went to my bedroom and unpacked my things. I checked my closets, all of my dresses were there, skirts, blouses, it was heaven to see so many lovely things. I took off my school uniform, the blouse, miniskirt and pantyhose and put on my black silk shirtdress and checked myself in the mirror, it sure looked good. It suddenly struck me that wearing this dress almost by accident had started off this whole crazy rollercoaster ride. A feeling of doubt and panic shot through me, had I let everyone push me into this, something I didn't want. But I looked back at the pretty girl in the black silk dress and thought of my days at school, my friends, even the way I felt about myself and my life. What I'd said to Ellen had been true, I was overjoyed at what had happened to my life.

Mom took me to the hospital the following morning

and we saw the consultant. He seemed nice, questioned me about how I felt. "What about hormones, Miss Hague, how many are you taking?"

When I told him he appeared to be impressed.

"That is a high dose, you're obviously almost entirely female already. I can see that, of course, I'm certainly not blind."

He called my mom back in. "She's definitely ready for the surgery, Mrs. Hague. I've got good news, we've got a vacant slot, she can be admitted right now and I can do the operation tomorrow."

We looked at each other, astounded. I felt my world falling out beneath my feet again, I'd happily thought this was just another part of a long journey and there would be some time before the actual operation was done, but stay here now and be operated on tomorrow?

"I think that's a good idea, honey," Mom said. Get it over with and you won't have to worry during the waiting. Go ahead and do it."

The consultant looked at me. "You're sure?"

I felt myself nodding. In a daze I signed some forms and a nurse came into the office, my mom kissed me goodbye and wished me luck and the nurse led me away.

When I got into bed I was shaking with fear, the consultant came in to check and prescribed a shot that sent me straight to sleep. Early next morning I had a dim recollection of being prepared for surgery and then I was unconscious again. I woke up in a great deal of numbness and pain from my crotch, my breasts hurt too. Mom and Dad were there.

"How do you feel, honey?" Dad asked.

"Ok, I guess. When are they doing the operation?"

"It's done," Mom laughed. "You are now completely and in every way female."

I gaped at her and looked down at my breasts.

"Why do they hurt?"

"They were enlarged, honey, remember you wanted to be a thirty eight C? Now you are."

She told my father to go out of the room and then helped me to see my breasts. They were still in dressings and felt sore, but they really were bigger. I smiled when I saw them. I asked her to call Dad back in.

"Thanks, Mom, thanks Dad."

CHAPTER TEN

Andrew and Ellen stayed with us over Christmas, they were both fascinated that I'd actually done it and really was fully female now in every way. The hormones, diet and corseting had done their work and instead of having to be laced into the heavy corset each day I could wear pretty basques and waspies. Each time I looked at my nude body, I couldn't help touching and feeling my tits, they looked perfect to me, larger and beautiful, I knew the scars would quickly heal. My crotch hurt like hell, there was no question, but it eased as each day passed. Mom helped me to bathe and dress my new sore parts, she seemed to have a vitality and enthusiasm with her new daughter that I hadn't seen before, she took care of me like a little girl. Dad had slipped easily into his role, spending time with Andrew and leaving Mom and me to do what mom's and their daughters do the world over. After ten days, the dressings were removed at the hospital and my new vagina was introduced to the world. That evening I was in the bath, soaking in a mix of antiseptic and bath bubbles when Mom came in. She sat and chatted for a while, occasionally looking anxiously at me. Was it my tits, I wondered, was something not right? In the end I couldn't stand it anymore.

"Mom, for heaven's sake, tell me what's on your mind."

She looked at me guiltily. "Er, could I take a look Sarah?"

"Look? At what?"

"Your new vagina. I'm sorry but I'm your mom, I do need to see that everything is as it should be."

I laughed. "Of course you can, let me get out of the bath and I'll come into my bedroom."

I toweled off and went to see Mom. I lay on the bed, drew up my feet under my knees so that my vagina was open for her to see. She looked at it minutely for a couple of minutes.

"It's perfect, darling, I'm so pleased. I thought it might look, well, you know, artificial."

"Mom, don't be silly. Of course it's fine."

I put on my pretty purple dress and tied the sash, touched in my face and tidied my hair and then went down to spend an hour with my parents before bed. Andrew and Ellen had gone back to New York and we spent a quiet evening, just the three of us. I felt entirely comfortable, I was sure that they did too.

"You go back to school on Sunday, darling," Mom said abruptly.

"I know, Mom. I'll be ready. You're taking me?"

"No, Hannah's mom will do the honors again. You remember last time, the first time you went to Karen Hall?"

"Yeah, I do Mom, I was terrified, on the way I was going to persuade you to turn around and bring me home and put a stop to it all."

"We thought you would be planning something like that, your father and I discussed it and asked Mrs. Blake to take you instead, we rather thought you'd be less likely to pull something like that with her."

We all laughed. "I'm glad you did it that way and I went to Karen Hall," I told them. "It's worked out well, I love it there."

"You like being a schoolgirl?" Dad said to me.

I had to think for a moment. "Yes, of course I do Dad, why wouldn't I?"

I got backto Karen Hall after Christmas. I went up to our room and Hannah was waiting for me, she gave me a kiss and helped me unpack. She was strangely quiet, and I couldn't work out what the problem was.

"Is everything ok, Hannah, you're ok?"

"Oh yes, of course, I'm fine."

"And we're ok, you don't want to share a room with

someone else?"

"No, of course not, that's ridiculous."

"Then for God's sake, tell me what's on your mind, why are you looking so weird?"

She'd gone bright red with embarrassment and couldn't even speak. Then I remembered my mom, her fascination with how my operation turned out.

"Hannah, I'm going to take a shower. After, I'll come out with nothing on and you can see my new tits and cunt, is that what's on your mind?"

She colored even brighter red but nodded and smiled.

"Yes, it is, I'm sorry, but I'd love to take a peek."

I stripped off and took a shower, before I went into the bathroom she stepped forward to unlace my corset but smiled when she saw that I wore a simple basque that I could unfasten myself. I didn't take my panties off, I didn't want her to see yet, but she noticed my larger tits and her mouth opened.

"Sarah, they're gorgeous."

"Yeah, I'm quite keen on them too."

I came out of the shower, lay on the bed with my feet under my knees and she inspected my cunt minutely. Like my mom, she was impressed with the work the surgeon had done.

"Did it hurt much?" she asked me.

"Yeah, it did, imagine having a slice of you cut off. But it's ok now, I take pain killers and it's easing every day, I hardly notice it these days. I keep up with the hormones too of course."

"When will it be ready for action?" she asked.

"I reckon another month should do it, but don't worry, we can keep going the way for now."

She bent down and kissed me and I felt myself melting with warmth and desire for this beautiful young girl. We were so alike that I never wanted our relationship to end, although I guessed it would have to one day. We made love, or at least I made love to her, I was still feeling too bruised to have her touching me too intimately. We slept together, hugging our young female bodies tightly in the same bed. In the morning we dressed in blouses and gymslips and went down to start classes.

That afternoon there was a meeting in the hall and we received our results for the previous trimester. We'd scored highly, very highly. We'd done so well that I became head girl and Hannah deputy head girl. We were given special badges to wear on our gymslips, blouses and blazers and were allowed extra privileges which included the use of a smaller common room set aside for the more senior girls. It was a dizzy time, on the Friday we went into town and bumped into the boys we'd met at the dance. Peter was insistent that we make a date so I agreed to see him the following evening. It was early days and besides, I genuinely wasn't interested in the poor guy but I didn't turn away when he 'accidentally' brushed past my tits.

"'I'm sorry, excuse me," he said.

I nodded and saw Hannah trying to keep a straight face. The following evening we met the boys again and this time while we were on the dance floor, smooching to a slow song, he did touch one of my tits and I let him. It was probably more a thrill for me than it was for him, the first time that a guy had actually found my new tits so enticing that he had to touch and fondle them. That was as far as I was going to let him go, period.

And so we worked through the trimester, keeping our heads down and studying hard to get the results we needed for Wellesley. Once, Hannah asked me curiously if I resented doing it, having already done it all once before.

"Not at all, remember, this is a first for Sarah, she's never done this before and anything that happened in a previous life is just a dream, it's of no interest to me. Besides, we became friends, if nothing had happened we'd never have known what we have now."

She gave me a gentle kiss and carried on with her studies.

I went home again for the Easter vacation. Mom was keen for me to have fun and let my hair down.

"After all, you want to experience being a girl, Sarah, you should go out and enjoy yourself. I know I did."

But I didn't, I enjoyed my life as it was, I didn't want to 'go out and enjoy myself'. All I wanted was a quiet holiday, catch up with a little work and read some books. All my previous life I'd read crappy macho stuff, now I was trying to catch up on what I'd missed, the English writers like the Brontes and Jane Austen, modern American women's literature, biographies of Jackie Kennedy and even Katharine Lee Bates, the well known Wellesley educator. When we got back to school I threw myself back into my work, as did Hannah.

I'd managed to grasp the essentials of netball, had signed up for hockey and was even taking tennis lessons. It seemed to me that the more I did the more active I was, the more I wanted to do. Was it the hormones, I wondered, but that seemed doubtful. Was it the surgery, which had now healed completely? That was illogical. There could only be one reason, for the first time in my life I was happy beyond reason, I was the person I should always have been. We got provisional places offered to us at Wellesley and went for a celebration, both of us got slightly drunk and had to sneak back into school by the back door. Eventually I went on to captain the hockey team and sent Mom and Dad a photo of me fronting the whole team. They came to school for graduation and I let them into our room. When we were ready we went back down stairs and they made me have my photo taken in my graduation gown. The photographer had an instant print system and he handed us three copies of the photo. I looked at it and saw a happy, smiling eighteen year old girl, slim, very pretty, elegant and proud. I looked at their faces and knew that they were too. When I went to receive my diploma they were in the second row and I saw them clearly, tears streaming down both their faces.

Our cases were packed and Dad took them and put them in the car. I said goodbye to Hannah and her mom and we parted, we agreed to meet up during the summer recess. We'd have a lot to catch up on and there was one thing that neither of us had done and both of us were burning with curiosity to do it. I hadn't been fucked in my new vagina, I'd been too wary after the pain of the operation and wanted to let it heal totally.

Back home, Andrew was already there for the vacation and Ellen was staying with him. When they saw the confident, pretty young woman who entered the house, shining with happiness and dressed to kill in a new designer summer dress, my hair styled to perfection and my makeup glowing, they didn't say a word for a few moments. Then Andrew said one word. "Well."

Well indeed, I wondered if it had worked out as well for him. Probably not. I went up to my room, Dad had put my case on the bed and I started unpacking. Did I want revenge on the two people that had been the architects of all of this? No, that would be stupid, they'd done me the biggest favor anyone could possibly have done for me. But when Ellen came into my room and looked at me, a gleam in her eye, I couldn't resist.

"Did you want a hand unpacking, Sarah?"

"Fuck off, Ellen," I said sweetly. Girls can be so cruel when they want to.

We had a good summer vacation, Mom took me shopping for new clothes, I needed some new stuff for when I went away to college. We were in a trendy, expensive boutique when she asked me quite naturally if I wanted to buy some jeans.

"Whatever for?" I asked her.

"To wear, of course, most girls wear jeans at some time."

"Not this girl, Mom, I like dresses and skirts. I want to buy something really pretty, not denim jeans."

Fortunately she wasn't wearing jeans, although she did on occasion, today she was wearing a dress like I was. We went into the next store and I saw her admiring a beautiful cocktail dress.

"Why don't you try it on, Mom, I think it would look really good on you."

"Do you think so?" she asked me.

"Absolutely."

She went into the changing room and came out wearing the cocktail frock, a dark red silk Versace that had a monstrous price tag but was reduced to an affordable level in the sales. She twirled around.

"Well?"

"It's really nice, Mom. Dad will love you wearing it."

She bought the dress, after all, I'd instinctively known

what would clinch it for her.

We waded through store after store and I wound up with expensive underwear, dresses, petticoats, a smart business suit, skirts, blouses, it was endless.

"I think you need a new raincoat, Missy, that polka dot one is a little bit on the young side for you now."

"Yeah, especially with the shiny rubber boots," I grinned.

I tried on several and we agreed on a short Michael Kors trenchcoat, it was well above the knees, beautifully made with a belt around the waist. When we got home we had a dozen packages for Dad to carry up the stairs to my bedroom. He grumbled, but when he saw Mom in the new cocktail dress his eyes lit up and all was forgiven.

A week before I was due to depart for Wellesley, Andrew asked to have a word with me. He'd been away for most of the summer on a trip with Ellen, but had come back alone. He didn't look well, I was very concerned about my older brother.

"Sis, I've got huge problems," he said anxiously.

"Nothing that we can't sort out, tell me what's bothering you and we'll see if we can't make some sense out of it."

"You've changed, you know," he said seriously.

I threw back my head and laughed. "Really, you noticed, did you? Of course I've changed, so have you."

"No, I mean more than that. Since you became a girl you've blossomed into a different person, confident, pretty, you know where you're going."

It was true, I explained to him how much I loved my new life. By association, of course, my old life was just the opposite, but it wouldn't do to tell him that.

"Well, I hope so, Andrew," I said to him. "I'm a girl now and I want to make the best of the rest of my life."

"Yeah. Did you know I had the surgery too?"

I shook my head. "No, nobody told me. Congratulations, then. You must be happy."

He shook his head. "Afterwards, Ellen and I went away for a vacation, I thought we'd start everything from scratch, we'd got what we both wanted. Then she left me, we broke up. I guess she's a lesbian."

I laughed. "Of course she's a lesbian, that's what she saw in you in the first place, before you changed."

"So you knew?"

"Yes, girls that make passes at other girls are usually that way inclined. She made…"

I tailed off.

"She made a pass at you then?"

I shook my head, saying nothing.

"Well, it's finished now anyway. I'm going back to Columbia, but I feel really lonely, did you feel that way at Karen Hall?"

"No, I didn't. Hannah was with me, of course, lots of other girls and I loved it almost from day one."

"So what do I do, Sis?"

He was in a hell of a state, overwrought, tense, he wasn't thinking straight at all. I thought about my own new life.

"Go back to Columbia, spend every waking moment on your studies, find a good friend, either gender, it doesn't matter. If you get any free time, take up some sport and play like hell."

"Is that what you did?"

"Yep, that was it, simple really, study like hell and play sports like hell. Andrew, you're a good looking guy, when you've done your work, chill out and let it all come to you."

He leaned over and kissed me on the cheek. "Thanks Sis, it sounds like good advice. It certainly worked for you."

"Just one thing before you go, Andrew."

"Yes?"

"Whatever else you do, stay out of my closet and keep your hands off my dresses, clear?"

He nodded. "Clear."

THE END

www.ingramcontent.com/pod-product-compliance
Lightning Source LLC
Chambersburg PA
CBHW020950071025
33679CB00010B/334